Opposite Directions

A Novel

Danny Ingram

This is a work of fiction. Similarities to real people, places, or events are entirely coincidental.

OPPOSITE DIRECTIONS

First edition. October 8, 2023.

ISBN: 979-8223352259

Written by DANNY Ingram.

ONE

It was a night unlike any other. And, our lives would never be the same.

In the year since the accident, our grief and our goals kept us on the straight and narrow. We really missed not going to the weekend parties and dances with our friends. Tonight was going to be different. We were going to reward ourselves with a little relaxation and fun, but in the quiet and cautious company of a couple of very close friends who were keeping it under wraps. It started out great. Just what we needed.

Smithville, in many ways, is a typical small town. There is one main road that runs through town with only one stop light. The local police department makes their budget quota on ticketing those passing through town who don't slow down to a crawl at 30 mph. There are no theaters, bowling alleys, or skating rinks. All of those things are in neighboring towns. Just about everything is locally owned. There's the BBQ pit, furniture store, liquor store, and burger shack along the highway, with churches, gas stations and homes scattered in between.

More mom and pop stores like the pharmacy, grocery store and the local insurance agent's office line Main Street and the post office anchors one end and the bank the other. The volunteer fire department sits just behind city hall, while a popular beer joint is just across the highway and behind the feed store.

A typical weekend of entertainment includes either going to the dancehalls, finding a party with a few kegs of beer out on someone's place in the country, or just driving up and down the highway and doing what is commonly called 'making the Y'.

We were all casual tonight since we didn't plan on seeing anyone else. Ben arrived to pick me up wearing blue jeans and Converse high tops—Chuck Taylors—with a Frampton Comes Alive concert t-shirt untucked and just a little tattered from wear and tear. The quarterback whose arm made me a good receiver, was just over 6' and a very solid

180. His ticket to paying for college was through the Marines, where he had a rich family history of service.

I got in the car so we could go pick up Reggie. I wore blue jeans with both knees ripped and looking in need of a good needle and thread. My Adidas low tops, this past season's basketball shoes were now a dull white from too many pickup games at the park and I had on one of my college recruitment t-shirts, this one from the Georgia Bulldogs.

Reggie was waiting for us outside in the driveway as we drove up to his house. A quiet guy, but a beast on the field, he was only about 160 and played guard on the offensive line—helping give Ben the time he needed to find me open and throw the me the ball. As nice a guy as you will find, he was tough as nails. Tonight, he wore pressed jeans, cowboy boots, and a green Izod shirt. Of course, we teased him, when in fact, it was he who should have been teasing us for our lazy and worn attire.

A damp mist hung in the late summer's night air and filled Ben's pride and joy, his Olds 442 he bought with savings from hauling hay each summer, with the heavy air. We drove with the windows down and not a care in the world, only the constant hum of cicadas competing with the Eagles' five-part harmony on *Peaceful Easy Feeling*.

Cruising the back roads and enjoying some cold ones for the past couple of hours, it was just before midnight as we headed back knowing it wouldn't be long before our friends would be driving back into town from the dance. It was the final night of the Fayette County Fair, a summer-ending event that nobody wanted to miss. Our escape to the country roads, some paved and many gravel, just outside of town was a first for me in a long time. We made sure to keep it quiet. There were good reasons I did not want to be seen out partying.

Passing the livestock auction barn as we eased our way back into town, we turned the volume down on Glenn Frey and made the Y—a drive up and then back down the highway that cuts through our little town and ends with traffic splitting off into two directions. The streets were quiet with the exception of our one police officer and a late-night trucker coming through town on the way to Houston.

This night was just what I needed, to finally get out of the house and enjoy a little freedom and fun driving around with friends.

Only a few blocks away from being dropped off at my house, I felt my phone vibrate and saw that it was Susan. I answered right away and heard these words.

"Hurry— before it's too late!"

Five words that were about to change our lives.

I had only heard this tone in her voice once before, and I quickly sobered up at the thought that she may be in trouble. Older than me by just over a year, Susan, strong-willed and fiercely independent, would never ask for help unless something was seriously wrong.

"What's up Susan? What's wrong?"

She continued in short bursts, trying her best to hold it together.

"I don't know how this happened. I can't believe it. I must have fallen asleep. This is going to cost me my scholarship. Where are you? Can you come help?"

"We just got back in town. We were headed home for the night. What happened and where are you!?"

"On Main Street. I wrecked your car into the train exhibit." Susan began to sob. Now there was no doubt—something was very wrong.

"I'll be there in two minutes."

Susan's call brought our quiet and laid-back night to an abrupt turnabout. Leaning forward to the front seat, I began barking directions to Ben and Reggie.

"Turn around! We've got to get downtown as fast as possible without anyone seeing us. Cross the highway by U-Totem and head over to First Street. That's the quickest way since there is only one intersection along the railroad tracks. We just saw Officer Logan, the new policeman, walking into the U-totem. That should buy us a little extra time."

"Alright! I'm on it. What's going on with Susan?" Ben shouted back over the sound of the wind whipping through the car windows and the hum of his 442's V8 engine as we sped across town. Ben knew exactly what to do, punching the Oldsmobile just enough to speed down the street but not unleash its full roar so as not to wake up those sleeping in the homes we passed on the way. As a close friend of Susan, he was worried about her.

Leaning even closer to Ben so he could hear me, I answered, "She says she crashed my car into the train exhibit."

"Is she hurt?"

"I don't think so, but I'm not sure. She really seems rattled."

Reggie piped in. "Oh wow—the timing on this sucks. She just got that big award and scholarship for her work on that exhibit. I hope she's okay. I hope this doesn't screw things up for her. We all know how y'all have sacrificed and what that scholarship means to her. "

Reggie was right, and now I became even more worried. "Step on it! We have got to help her."

It was ironic that this was the first night that either of us—Susan or me—had gone out since the tragic accident that left us on our own. We both had greater aspirations than a high-school education would afford us. We knew our only path forward was getting scholarships. So, we kept our noses to the grindstone determined to be disciplined enough to earn our college degrees. We were not non-drinkers or against it, and we would have loved to party like our friends through our high school years, but we knew our only path forward was getting scholarships and we were determined not to be derailed by any mistakes.

After many invitations over the years, we had decided that tonight was a good night to go out and just keep it quiet. Most everyone would be out of town at the fairgrounds for the dance. It was the last big dance of the year before school started and everyone made it a point to be there. Two of my close buddies, though, were more interested in hanging out with me for a few beers than going to the dance, and so this seemed like the perfect time. Susan made her plans. I let her use my car, and I jumped in with my buddies, Ben and Reggie, and we all followed the plan to stay off the highway, on the backroads, and out of sight in case anyone came home early from the dance.

Now, all of a sudden, the night flipped from good to bad—really bad.

Ben was the first to see it. "Oh man! That doesn't look good. Your car is sitting in what used to be the lobby of the museum, and it's against the rail car".

"There's Susan. Stop the car over here," I said as I jumped out and ran over and gave her a big hug.

Susan was tall with an athletic build. Her shoulder length brown hair was pulled back in a tight pony tail. Her brown eyes glistened in the night light that blended into her dark summer tan. She didn't plan to see anyone else tonight, so just had on flip flops, short white shorts and a t-shirt, with gold earrings and a matching necklace and bracelet.

"Are you okay?"

"Yes. I think I just fell asleep while I was driving. I don't remember hitting this." Susan's cries turned into soft sobs.

"Okay, let's figure this out. We don't have a lot of time. Ben and Reggie, let's see if we can get this car started, or at least push it out of here".

Working furiously to push the car off the train and out of the building, the three of us gave it our all while Susan kept trying to start the car. Nothing was working. The car would not budge—it was stuck on something that we just couldn't see—and it wouldn't start. Time was running out.

This antique rail car museum is considered a town treasure. It lights up the south end of Main Street with prominent signs throughout the town displaying its rich history. With the railroad as a backdrop, this 'one-of-only-three-in-the-world' rail car is a point of pride for the town. The unique rail car was acquired by local philanthropists Henry and Sissie Crawford and shipped to Smithville from Rome. The museum built around it was funded through a grassroots community campaign with virtually every family of this rural community pitching in a little something, giving everyone the feeling of ownership. It had become intrinsic to the town's identity.

Still making no progress, I felt time was running out. "We can't wait any longer. Someone, probably the police, is going to drive by and sees us."

Ben wasn't ready to give up. "We can keep trying. We have to. This is not going to end well as much as everyone loves this train and museum."

I really appreciated my friend's willingness to do whatever we could to get out of this situation.

But, after another five minutes of no movement, I couldn't wait any longer. I had to get Susan out of there.

"That scholarship and Susan's reputation with the Heritage Society are the most important things to protect right now. Here's what I need you and Reggie to do. Please take Susan home. I'll keep doing what I can to get this car out of here, but I don't want Susan or either of you—after drinking tonight, to get caught up in any trouble. I know it's asking a lot, and I really appreciate y'all. But, please, get out of here now. I'll be fine."

There was no argument this time. Ben and Reggie got Susan into their car. They agreed that she needed to be protected. And, besides, their good buddy Frank always found a way to get things done.

"Thanks so much Frank. We both are going to owe you a big one," Reggie yelled with his head out the window and looking back as the Olds 442 kicked up dust from the gravel parking lot.

As their tail lights faded into the night, I went back to work trying to free my car—and now myself—from this mess. I tried again and finally got the car to start. I tried everything I could think of to get it to rock forward, backwards, turning the wheels, anything but the car would not move. I got out and crawled under the car again and finally saw what was keeping it from moving. The front bumper was hooked on the train's steps. I crawled under, was able to use my legs with leverage against the door railing that had been broken off and bend the fender back enough to free it. Just another minute and I would be out of there. As I crawled out from underneath the car, headlights appeared on the ground before me and then blinding in my face. It was Officer Logan, the new cop in town.

"Excuse me son. What in the hell is going on here?" Logan was new to town, so I didn't know him and he didn't know me either. I started to answer, but it was obvious he was being a smart ass and did not expect nor want an answer.

"Put your hands out where I can see them and turn around slowly and place them on the trunk of the car. You, son, are under arrest."

Five more words that would change my life forever.

TWO - Twenty Years Later

Driving into my hometown triggers feelings of nostalgia. Passing the VFW reminds me of the times we played under the giant 100-year old oak tree and chasing lizards on the large outdoor pavilion. Crossing the river bridge brings back memories of playing under the bridge and swimming off the boat ramp. And then there is the town's big water tower greeting the travelers as they enter the town. Each of these things seem to spark different memories.

Small towns don't really change, and when they do it's very gradual. But, it's been 20 years since I moved away, so I notice quite a few changes. Not the least being that the "Y" is now a "T" with another traffic light. My little town now has two traffic lights. Do the kids now "make the T" like we used to make the Y?

However, today my mind quickly drifts away from nostalgia.

A slow, steady rain begins to fall. The automatic wipers clear the windshield. Just past the old Mobil station, one street past Main, I turn and drive up the street a couple of blocks. The gravel-crunching sound of the tires entering the parking lot finds me as the first car to arrive. This is not something I would ever look forward to, but I hurry across the street and into the building as the skies grow darker and the rain begins to pour down.

I find myself sitting inside a building that I've been to many times. It's a somber place. People enter, shaking the rain off their clothes as they fill the seats. There are quiet whispers of conversations throughout the building that grow louder as the crowd grows larger. Seated on the front row, I can't really see who all has come this afternoon.

It's time. I knew this was going to be hard, but I had no idea how hard it would be. Standing, I straighten my tie and button my coat, tug the sleeves of my pressed white button down moving the cuffs out from under my coat. I walk, slowly and purposefully, to the front of the room. I compose myself and face the group before me.

Today, the secret we had to live with for these past twenty years, ends. It was a sacrifice well worth making, even though I went from being a hometown hero to villain overnight. I am not sure what reaction I'm about to get, even though it doesn't matter, since I am positive nobody in this place is here because I am speaking.

It's a large gathering in an intimate space. The first words out of my mouth come out a little shaky, but I quickly steady myself and continue. Public speaking is routine for me, but the emotion of this moment—in giving a eulogy for someone you love—is not.

"Let me first say thank you to each of you for being here today. Days like this are difficult for all of us. None of us want to be here. It's very kind of you to make the time to honor Susan."

Susan was everyone's friend, rising above all the animosity towards me and becoming a pillar of the community with her support of all things local. Today they filled the pews of this quaint, mid-century building that is dimly lit, even for a funeral home chapel on a stormy afternoon. The room is eerily quiet except for the sound of creaking pews and the rain, which is now pounding down on the roof.

"Susan loved all of you—her tennis group, the book club gang, all of her fellow volunteers from school and church, and most of all the Heritage Society members. Thank you for loving her and her caring spirit. She was a smart, funny, athletic, and loving person who was my best friend—and my sister. She faced her struggles over these last years with grace and perseverance.

We loved growing up in this small town. Not much more than a year apart, we were each other's biggest supporters. We had to be after we lost our family in a tragic accident. But, I know we would have been close no matter what the circumstances. Growing up, we did everything together, whether it was sports or hiking or just hanging out with friends. I have so many favorite memories growing up with her. We were confidants and mentors to each other. When we lost our parents, it wasn't easy but we knew we would be okay because we had each other.

We were our own little family. And, you—her closest friends—she also considered you part of her family.

I have no doubt that each of you have stories you could tell that will make us both laugh and cry. I've got a few of my own to tell, but please come up and share yours, as well. As sad as her story ended, hearing these stories can make us all feel better—and that's exactly what Susan would have wanted."

THREE

While her friends shared stories of their love and affection for Susan, it was obvious that they did not feel that way about me. No surprise. Not wanting to hang around long after the ceremonies finished, I thank as many of her friends as I can, at least those that don't literally turn their back to me. All of them have been so kind to her throughout her life, but especially at the end. There are quite a few I feel like I know from my conversations with Susan over the years. Many of them are people that moved to town well after I left and so it's my first time to actually meet some of them. I can tell they've heard the stories around town about me, and while doing so cautiously, at least are willing to give me the courtesy of paying their respects to my sister. We all know we lost Susan quite some time ago to this terrible disease and have just been waiting for this day to come and release her from all her pain. These last months, it was only machines that kept her alive. We all said our personal good-byes earlier.

Anxious to leave, I begin making my way to the door. I notice that "Little Roger" Daniels, one of my coach's sons who was five years behind me in school, appears to be waiting to talk to me just outside the door. And, it looks like "Little Roger" is not so little anymore. At 6'4" and about 190 pounds, his muscular frame is accentuated by an ill-fitting suit, probably a size or two too small, and his close-cropped red hair.

"Frank," he says walking up to me and shaking my hand. "I am very sorry for your loss. I know we weren't close since I was just in junior high when you graduated, but I want you to know I always appreciated how you took time to speak to me and my friends as we hung around your practices and in the Field House after games. I know part of it was because Dad was the coach, but you didn't have to do that. I don't remember many of your teammates giving us the time of day. But, I also want you to know it wasn't just about trying to emulate you in sports.

I always looked up to you and admired how you and your sister were so close. You never hid that fact just out of bravado and trying to look cool. It was a good lesson for me, and I tried to follow your lead—not only on the field or court—but in how I treated my sister. And, today, just like you mentioned when you were talking about Susan, my sister and I are best friends because of it."

I was smiling because he was really on a roll, but when Roger paused to take a breath, I took the chance to thank him for his kind words. Coach Daniels had told me how Roger really looked up to me and wanted to be an athlete, wear the same number as me and play the same positions. It was humbling to me, especially at that young age, to know he saw me as a role model.

"You still look like you could play today. You look the same—still about 6'4" and 220 or so—the same as you were your junior year when you won just about every award there was for football, basketball, and track?"

I laughed, especially because he even knew my height and weight when I was in high school. "You're awful nice to say that. Even though I was away at college when you played, I am fully aware that you broke many of my records and won your share of awards, as well. Congratulations on that. And, Roger, thanks for staying behind and talking to me. It's been good to see you and to catch up a little. Please give your dad my regards."

I'll always owe Little Roger's dad a debt of gratitude. He was one of the very few who stood behind me and supported me after my arrest. Most people in town quickly jumped on the bandwagon of 'guilty until proven innocent'. But, the coaches believed in me. They listened to and accepted my apology. Their support and understanding turned out to be critical. I knew they had to suspend me from all athletics for my senior year due to a longstanding and well-known rule for all athletes—if arrested, you're automatically suspended.

I worried this would probably ruin any chances of getting a scholarship and going to college. But, the coaches spent many hours over the past few years around me and knew my true character. They believed in me and knew my true character. They stood up for me when college recruiters brought up their concerns after my arrest. A few schools did withdraw their scholarship offers, but most did not. Thanks to the coaches, good grades, and luckily enough talent—even though suspended for my senior year the recruiting services rated me as one of the top prospects. This allowed me to accomplish my goal getting a scholarship and graduating from college.

The sacrifices Susan and I had made paid off for both of us, even if we did make it a little more difficult by screwing up that one fateful night.

I shook Roger's hand again and was about to leave when Roger had one more thing to add.

"Look, I know you took a lot of heat for what happened and that people in this town turned on you, but I believe you got a raw deal. And, I'm not the only one who feels this way. I just want you to know that all that stuff is now being brought up again by your old friend Dennis Johnson. Y'all were classmates. He's now our county judge and is just trying to deflect criticism about himself. He's had two DUI's and says he is going to run for office next year. So, after all these years he's bringing up the past and trying to avoid the talk about his drinking. Honestly, I don't know why, but Susan's passing seems to have set him off and folks at the beer joint say he's been saying he's got some kind of information and is going to take you down."

Not sure whether Roger is just being dramatic, I don't ask him to go into detail, but look him in the eye as I take my car keys out of my pocket. "That's really strange. Thanks for the heads up. Now I really have to go so I can catch an early morning flight."

Well, it seems I still had one supporter in Roger after going from hero to villain. I took the fall and nobody ever knew why. I never regretted it. Susan never forgot it and could never talk to me without thanking me. It was a big hurdle in life, but one that I eventually cleared and it was in the past. Now, with Susan gone, I was the only one left who really knew what happened—so the burden of keeping the secret should end today. Whatever Dennis was up to, I didn't care.

With that, I cross the street, dodging the puddles of water left standing after the afternoon thunderstorm, and walk to the car. My rental this time is the same as every time, a Toyota Highlander Premiere edition. My assistant knows to always request it because it's the same as the vehicle I own. The familiarity is important because it allows me to just get in and drive without having to learn a different car's controls and systems. I learned early on when getting just any rental, that learning that model's systems for lights, which side the gas tank is on, and how to find all these in the dark of early mornings or night was an inconvenience easily overcome by simply asking for the same vehicle I already knew.

On my way out of town, I drive out to the cemetery one more time. I notice a red truck that seems to be following me. It drives through the second gate as I go through the first. It parks about 100 yards away under a big oak tree. I never see anyone get out. It feels a little unusual, but then everything about this day did. I doubt it was Dennis, and I wasn't going to let my conversation with Roger get into my head and get paranoid now.

Ignoring it, I stop to pay my respects. Only this time, I am not walking over to Susan's grave. I go to the gravesites of some of my best friends—Ben and Reggie. The secret is buried. There is nothing now that could happen to damage their reputations.

FOUR

The drive back to Austin is beautiful. Normally, reminiscing with "Little Roger", maybe it's time to stop calling him that, would leave a smile on my face. Under normal circumstances, his upbeat and joyful nature, not to mention all the compliments, should make me feel better. But, it's hard to feel good about anything today.

Driving through rolling hills, pastures dotted with grazing cattle, and into the beautiful Lost Pines forest brings back more memories like the family picnics with Susan and I roasting marshmellows with my mom and fishing with my dad. Today, though, would be a long, quiet ride as my mind shifted from memories to my future. I am numb to my surroundings. Even with the time to prepare, Susan's death hit me harder than I imagined. I am alone.

FIVE

So long ago, I don't remember when
That's when they say I lost my only friend
Well they said she died easy of a broken heart disease
As I listened through the cemetery trees...The Wallflowers

Still half asleep, my phone rings and startles me. I quickly realize its DB's ringtone and answer. DB is my right hand, my executive assistant. She calls every morning to review my schedule and makes sure I'm prepped and have what I need to get started on the day ahead.

DB Garcia moved rapidly from an entry-level position in our company and quickly worked her way up the corporate ladder. Loyal and hard-working, her family depends on her as the bread-winner to get her children through college without being overwhelmed with student loan debt.

Petite with auburn hair, sun-kissed with lighter streaks reaching her shoulders, her constant smile and happy demeanor exude confidence and energy. DB was a standout high school volleyball player known for her grit and determination, something she felt was an important attribute due to her size. Labeled by recruiters as being too small, Division I program scholarship offers never came. She carries this chip on her shoulder well, using it in positive ways to manage the competitive fire still burning inside to prove others wrong and succeed in all that she takes on. We have a lot in common.

DB first caught my attention while subbing for her boss, who retired during a major project I was leading. Needing a new executive assistant, I became so impressed with DB throughout the project that I took a chance on her. Against Human Resources' advice, I hired her to work for me, even though the other candidates had much more experience. It was a big jump for her not just in salary, but also in responsibility. And she felt the pressure from her peers who thought she was promoted too fast.

DB grew into the role quickly and soon stood out among all the executive assistants throughout the company. Her blend of smart and sassy, sweet but direct and firm, and fierce loyalty makes us a great team.

"I know yesterday was tough for you, so I let you sleep in a little longer than usual," DB said. "Your conference call for this morning has been rescheduled, so you are free until you leave for the airport around noon."

Feeling great relief, kind of like you did when school was cancelled for snow days in Texas, I replied, "Hey, DB—thanks so much."

DB had one quick note before we hung up. "When I was checking your voicemail, there was a weird message—kind of a drunken rant or threat."

"What about?"

"Well, I normally would have just deleted it and written it off as a nut case. But, the caller mentioned Susan's name and something about you paying for it."

I had planned to cover this later with her, when I was back at the office, but I gave DB a brief synopsis of the conversation I had with Roger before leaving the funeral home yesterday. "I really don't think it's anything to worry about. This former high school classmate of mine has bad-mouthed me for years. I'm told he has a drinking problem so it was most-likely just a drunken rant. However, to my knowledge, he's never had one bad thing to say about Susan. That's what's strange, along with the fact I have not seen nor talked to him in so many years. Let's not worry about this unless we hear anything more. With the schedule we have in front of us, including the Hawaii trip and the UT ceremony coming up, we don't have time for any distractions."

"Okay boss, I'm sure it's nothing but I wanted to let you know. Enjoy your morning and I'll see you back at the office tomorrow."

"I think I'll grab some coffee and breakfast tacos and make my way over to campus. I need to touch base with Dean Smith anyway about the ceremony, and you know I enjoy getting back on the Forty Acres when I'm in Austin."

Awake now and happy knowing that DB was taking care of me once again by freeing up my schedule so I could have some much-welcomed free time, I go on a long run on the Town Lake Hike and Bike Trail.

While the city has changed the name to Lady Bird Lake, honoring the late First Lady, and changed the trail's name to the Ann and Roy Butler Hike and Bike Trail in honor of a local former mayor and his wife, people who live here and those of us with some roots here still use the original name. The popular 10-mile trail runs along the lakeshore looping around and through parks and downtown high-rises. It's a Chamber of Commerce point of pride. Every day, rain or shine, you will find locals and tourists enjoying the beauty of this national gem in the heart of Texas.

I stop after seven miles, down a Gatorade and then grab a cup of coffee and walk back to the hotel. After a shower, I pack for the airport. Grabbing my wallet and keys I leave in search of Austin's finest breakfast tacos. Breakfast tacos are like live music in Austin—you can find them everywhere and anytime.

SIX

The University of Texas campus is commonly referred to as *The Forty Acres*. The nickname comes from the original "College Hill" on the campus. In reality, the State's premier university, established in 1883, is 437 acres in size. You know the saying—everything is bigger in Texas.

A majestic setting, it's one of the largest universities in the US. With seven museums, seventeen libraries, 50,000 students and almost 25,000 faculty and staff, it is an idyllic setting and an atmosphere you expect from a college campus. Every time I walk on campus, I still feel the energy and excitement that I first felt as a student.

My Uber driver drops me in front of the new McCombs Business School building. The college is consistently rated among the nation's top five or six business schools. This is my first look at my former school's new addition, a $200 million state-of-the-art building with classrooms and conference space that anchor the southwestern edge of campus. It makes a bold statement set among the neo-classical design and limestone buildings with orange-tiled roofs that make up the rest of campus.

During the grand opening ceremony, one reporter described it as a handsome brick and limestone façade that forms a prominent gateway to the campus. Another was amazed by the openness and beauty of the sparkling interior and glassy inner perimeter.

When asked for comment, competing schools accused The University of Texas of trying to keep up with the Joneses by adding this extravagant addition. The university spokesperson replied very matter of factly, "we don't try to keep up with the Joneses, we are the Joneses." There is nothing like some good 'ol Texas bravado.

Carefully holding two bags full of hot, freshly made breakfast tacos, I walked into the Dean's Office. There is no better way to make and keep friends than sharing an Austin breakfast taco, and I enjoy putting smiles on the faces of the dedicated staff who work in this office.

"Frank, what a pleasant surprise," Dean Smith calls out from his corner office, as he walks toward me. He puts his arm around my shoulder, expresses his condolences on my sister's death, and begins to walk with me as I greet his staff with breakfast tacos.

Dean Smith, dressed in a burnt orange polo, dark jeans, and wearing brown dockers loves when there are no major functions scheduled and he can drop the suit and tie and dress casually.

His silver waves of hair curled above his collar, and a trim silver beard give him a distinguished look. Time on the tennis courts has left his skin bronzed but healthy looking.

"Sorry to interrupt, but I had a meeting cancelled and while I was in town I just wanted to stop in and say hello," I replied. "I hope you were pleased with the results of the campaign."

Building new classrooms is not an inexpensive proposition. I convinced my board to give a contribution, and I pledged to match it. I am not one of the largest donors, but being an alum of the school, they treat me like one.

"We could not have finished the building project on schedule without your wonderful gifts. I can't thank you enough," continued Dean Smith.

"You have already thanked me enough, and I really appreciate it. The news release that you sent to all the business and trade publications created a lot of awareness for our company and got the story in front of many of my colleagues and clients. And, I love how the short video on the school's website turned out. I just wanted to stop in and say hi. Sorry this visit is so brief, but I have an airplane to catch." And with that, I handed out the last tacos and said my good-byes to the staff.

As we were walking to the door, I said, "Dean, I'll be back soon, the award ceremony is just around the corner."

"Yes, I need to talk to you about that. Let me walk with you so we can have a word in private."

Dean Smith let me know that the President's Office had received a call last night and the voice mail was potentially disturbing. I told him of the call to my office, and gave him the background on who and what I thought this was about. "Should I be worried about any risk to the university?"

"I'm sure, like you, that it's nothing", said Dean Smith. "The voice mails seem to match so it appears to be the same person. However, the president's policy is that all calls like this get a thorough investigation. They have to do their due diligence. I'll let them know what you just told me."

"Okay, thanks. I don't want to cause any problems for the university. If for some reason this becomes an issue with the award, please be honest and let me know."

"Don't worry now, I'll let you know if there is anything to be concerned about after I meet with the president. I'm on my way now to a meeting with President Adams and our executive team. We are meeting one of our new members of the President's Council for a final interview. If selected, and this is really just a formality with a final interview, the President has made it clear this is his choice, she will be installed at the same meeting you are receiving your award.

It is a beautiful fall day with a clear blue sky and a gentle, cool breeze. The lawns are still green since the first frost doesn't arrive until late November at the earliest. The flowers are beginning to fade and the leaves changing colors and falling to the ground. There are a lot of new buildings dotting the campus, but so many things have remained the same. The Tower and Main Building remain the centerpiece of campus. The Victorian-styled Main Building, commonly referred to as Old Main, is home to the famous UT Tower. The Tower stands at 307' and rises 27 floors. It is one of the most recognizable symbols of the university and the city.

Just down the steps from Old Main sits a group of classrooms nicknamed the Six Pack. It's view past the Littlefield Fountain and to the Texas State Capitol is stunning. Squirrels scurry around the lawn that sits between the buildings collecting acorns and looking for a handout from the students sitting out on the lawn with their backpacks. One thing all incoming freshmen students learn early is that on the UT campus there are six buildings—Batts Hall, Benedict Hall, Calhoun Hall, Mezes Hall, Parlin Hall, and Homer Rainey Hall—that line the South Mall leading up from the Littlefield Fountain towards the Tower. Everyone commonly refers to it as The Six Pack. Many students will have classes in one of these buildings, so it's a running joke that when they tell their parents their next class is in The Six Pack, there is usually some explaining to do.

I am really distracted and can't stop thinking about the voicemails. Am I taking this seriously enough if it could jeopardize my standing with the university? What has Susan's death got to do with this strange behavior if it is Dennis, my old classmate, that is doing this? A good walk will help me get my mind off of this.

Walking across campus, means traversing hilly terrain, as it sits on the edge of the Texas Hill Country. I don't have much time, but since I've been training for another triathlon I decide I will have no trouble getting around quickly. Starting at the Drag, the main street that sits on the western border of campus and student housing in what is referred to as West Campus, I notice that there are fewer 'mom and pop' stores than I remember. There are more chain retail, restaurants, and street vendors. I make my way north to see the new Moody College of Communication building, and then down Dean Keeton Dr. eastward by the Cockrell School of Engineering and south on Robert Dedman Dr. that runs between the LBJ Presidential Library and the legendary DKR stadium. The stadium now seats more than 103,000 football fans and the university continues to add more seats to the South end zone. From DKR, I climb the hills in central campus, passing by the Student Activity Center as I make my way by the old Gregory Gym and on to the West Mall. Even with my long run this morning, I make the walking tour faster and easier than I thought I would, so I'm a little early to meet the Uber that will take me to the airport.

Walking into the West Mall of the University of Texas campus, you are immediately engulfed in the ideology of universities and their students. Tree covered sidewalks stand in the shadow of the UT's infamous Tower. It's a beautiful shaded area of campus. It is also a route for the heaviest foot traffic from students crisscrossing campus to walk to their classes as they pass by tables, booths, and even a few activists standing with their guitars or tambourines lining the sidewalks. World hunger, anti-war and other social, political, religious, and health issues are represented, as well as student clubs, sororities, and fraternities. Just on the mall's edge, you may even find a group of Hari Krishna singing and dancing across the street from a street preacher warning the young adults of their sins of debauchery. And all these diverse groups exist in harmony, a far cry from the 'real world' outside of a college campus.

The West Mall holds many fond memories from my years as a student. This place sparks one memory in particular that has for years revisited me over and over again. Standing here immediately takes me back in time. This memory is relentless. I'm not normally a "what if?" person. I like to look forward. But, this one nags at me unlike anything. It just feels like something is not right, that something is unfinished. But, I keep filing it away as something that was just not meant to be.

SEVEN

It was my final semester and I had volunteered to lead a petition drive on the West Mall. As president of my Business School's student organization, I led a group of business majors asking other students to support a public policy that would level the playing field by creating new trade agreements with foreign competitors.

Ironically, the table next to us was an environmental cause blaming US businesses for polluting the air and water. We were all young students passionate about our own causes, but also friendly and in no way did we hold any animosity toward each other. We were just learning to exercise our right of free speech. It was a different time when everyone could do their own thing and be respected for it, and not be vilified as happens too often in today's society.

The wind was wreaking havoc on a canopy the environmental group was trying to set up. I went over to help and after a few minutes of helping hold it steady for a few working furiously to secure it, they were set and ready to start handing out their brochures. After a few minutes of small talk, I went back to my table. But, I found myself repeatedly glancing over at one of the girls in the group I had just met.

She kept catching my eye, and I hers, as the morning passed. There was something about her. Short with long brown hair and fair skin with olive tones, I could tell, since I was able to overhear from the close distance of our tables, that she was smart and had some spunk. I watched as she interacted with students passing by, some brushing her off as they hurried to class. But, she showed determination and persistence in getting their attention. I watched with great interest as her fellow student volunteers followed her lead. I probably should have been paying more attention to my own table. The volunteer shift was ending and I saw a chance and had to take it.

"Hi, I'm Frank," I said, walking over and introducing myself. "I see we are both finishing up our shifts. I'm headed over to the business school, how about coffee in the Atrium?"

"Oh, hi," she said, "I could really use a cup of coffee, but I'm going in the opposite direction. I've got to be at Kinsolving in 10 minutes." Kinsolving is one of the largest dormitories and is located on the northern edge of campus. The business school is on the opposite end.

I tried not to show my disappointment. "How about a rain check for coffee another day? Your name is ..."

"Sorry!", she interrupted. "I'm Sara. It's nice to meet you Frank. I really need to go so that I'm not late, but coffee another time would be nice."

As I watched her walk away, an odd feeling came over me. I was a little surprised by my reaction since I would just normally blow something like this off. After a second, I did shake it off and started on my way to the business school. There was something different about Sara. I could not stop thinking about her for the rest of the day.

A couple of hours later, I finished my work for a class project and closed my laptop for the day. It hit me and I suddenly realized that we had not exchanged phone numbers. How was I going to find her among the 50,000 UT students? I didn't even have her last name.

A little self-doubt crept into my mind, which is not like me at all. She said she was in a hurry. Did she say yes to coffee, but not really mean it? By rushing off, was she getting away from me before I asked her for her number? That evening I was restless all night over a girl I had just met, barely at that.

I thought I may find her, or at least someone who knows her, so returned the next day and there she was at the West Mall working for her environmental cause. I teased her about it and she assured me that she wasn't avoiding me and really did have to rush off. She seemed genuinely happy that I came back to find her, and we went and had coffee.

Jake's is a hole-in-the-wall coffee shop on the Drag, and a short walk from the West Mall. The place was empty so there was no wait as we got our coffees and sat down in the corner by the front window. Sara ordered a cappuccino with cinnamon powder. I got a drip coffee from Jake's Dark Roast selection. Jake's was the perfect place for us with its very relaxed atmosphere. We enjoyed our conversation and learned that we had so much in common, even if we differed on many issues in our separate fields of study. We stood on different sides of issues when it came to business versus the environment. But, from politics to sports and from music to food, we seemed to be in sync. We really enjoyed each other's company and spent a lot of the time laughing.

We went on a few dates, and got along great. But we had just as many dates cancelled because our schedules just kept conflicting. It was difficult finding time where one of us wasn't busy.

It was my last semester. I was already signed with McKay Consulting and would be leaving campus immediately after graduation to start my career in Boston as one of their analysts. Susan had just received her diagnosis and we needed money immediately. Since I was the only family she had, we knew that meant I needed to get a job right away. That weird, surprising emotion never left me when thinking about Sara, so I made sure to see her one last time before I left. We both agreed that maybe another time, or if we'd met earlier, things may have been different. She gave me a hug and a kiss. Even though we both agreed to not pursue a relationship any further, there was something powerful about our connection. But, it was decided and, being young and career focused, we convinced ourselves that it was just not meant to be.

Over the years, this memory just won't go away. We have never talked or seen each other since that day. I'm not sure why we didn't keep in touch, but maybe it was just too hard knowing we had strong feelings for each other. But, I've thought about Sara more often than I would have ever imagined.

EIGHT

I call DB on the walk over to meet my Uber that will take me to the airport.

"Hey DB—how's it going?"

"Good. Your conference call has been rescheduled for tomorrow and I'm now working on getting your Highlander reserved for next week. The rental company is trying to switch you to a Nissan and so we are going back and forth about it."

"Thanks for taking care of that. I do need your to help on something else."

"Sure, boss. What can I do to help you?"

I gave DB the background on my conversation with Dean Smith and the voice mail that came into the President's Office. "Will you see if you can find out more about Dennis Johnson? Don't spend a lot of time on it, I think a quick internet search may find what we need to know about him. Also, can you see if he drives a red pickup truck?"

"Sure, no problem. I'm assuming it was a red pickup that followed you to the cemetery?"

"Yeah, not that it means anything. But, it may be good to know in case he shows up around here and starts making threats. Thanks again. I'll see you tomorrow when I'm back in the office."

Hanging up and pinging the Uber driver, I thought about how grateful I am to work with such a good partner like DB.

NINE

Sara Cousins' plane arrived on time and she grabbed a cab and headed toward campus for her interview with the president. Driving in from the airport, she caught a glimpse of the Spanish tile roofs that frame the UT campus and minutes later she was stepping out and onto the campus for the first time in many years. The large oak trees provide a shaded canopy as she walks from her taxi driver's drop off by the Blanton Museum. Walking by Jester Hall and past McCombs School of Business, she takes the short cut by Batts Auditorium and comes out next to the Six Pack, facing its tree- lined promenade. She turns and faces the famous UT Tower, the iconic neoclassical clock tower structure where she would be meeting in a few minutes. It still looks the same, she thought to herself.

Walking up the steps of the South Mall, she feels the warm Texas sun as she steps out from the shade under the oaks and takes in the view. Ahead of her stands the Main Building and UT Tower. Behind her, a view down past the Littlefield Fountain and all the way to the Texas State Capitol building standing prominently on the hill. Taking it all in, Sara feels the memories flood back from her time on campus as a student. She thinks to herself that it has been way too long since she was last on campus, but that may be about to change. Just ahead is the West Mall, where she spent many days working the tables to create awareness for her favorite environmental causes.

It's a short walk across the mall, where she enters the grand building and takes the elevator to the 6th floor executive suites.

"Good morning, Ms. Cousins," President Adams said introducing himself as he steps out into the lobby outside his office. "It is a pleasure to finally meet you in person. I am really looking forward to our conversation. I've also included my executive team and they should all be arriving soon. While we wait for them, let me get us some coffee and we can chat."

Sara knew this was more interview than conversation, but appreciated his approach. "President Adams, I have heard good things about you and am happy to be here to talk with you about the council position. I am a proud alum and would be happy to serve my University, if you see fit, by bringing my background and experience to the council under your leadership".

Sara has had an all-star list of achievements since graduating and leaving the UT campus years ago. Along the way, she married a former law partner and they had made a nice life together. They had no children. She did pro bono work for many children's rights organizations. Her husband was diagnosed with pancreatic cancer, one of the cancers that have no way to be detected early. The stage four diagnosis meant that the treatment plan was not for a cure, but was to alleviate pain and suffering as long as possible. Sara had taken a lot of time away from work to spend the last months with her husband, and now it had been seven years where she had poured her heart and soul into her company and her work.

After the arrival of the executive team members and a chance for Sara to be introduced to each of them, the group finds their seats around the large oak table with a 360 view from the floor to ceiling windows as coffee was served. As President Adams is about to begin, Dean Smith arrives late and a quick introduction is made. President Adams continues by addressing the group with a typical summary of Sara's resume. Graduated with honors from the UT College of Liberal Arts, received her law degree from Harvard, interned for Supreme Court Justice Nelson, and was a managing partner in the nation's largest legal firm, Morris, McClure, and Newbury— better known as MM&N—before building and running her own world class firm, among too many other awards and achievements to note.

"You have represented the University so well throughout your distinguished career, so first of all let me just say thank you. Thank you for even considering this council position. I am well aware of your record and have spoken to many of your colleagues. Each of them says how lucky we would be to have you serve with us."

After about an hour of conversation, mainly listening to the president express his vision, Sara was officially offered the position. "This meeting is somewhat of a formality, in that I wanted to personally meet you and have you meet my team."

Sara was humbled by the president's words, and expressed what a privilege it was to be offered a seat on the President's Council.

"I am happy to accept your offer. Thank you," Sara replied as she stood to shake President Adam's hand.

With a short one-on-one conversation about her responsibilities and time commitments, Sara left the building feeling very happy. It was in times like these that she missed sharing good news with her husband. While it had been seven years since his death, she thought of him often and it always put a smile on her face. While the personal wounds of grief had healed, Sara had not found time for nor had the interest in dating. Her work had been 'the love of her life' but she was beginning to have second thoughts. She missed having someone to share her life with again.

It was the top of the hour, and the UT clock tower's chimes rang loudly as thousands of students made their way to and from classes in every direction, filling the entire main mall. In less than ten minutes, the mass of students was off the sidewalks and onto their destinations across campus. Sara looked up as a gap finally appeared and saw students standing behind tables in the West Mall, just as she had done as a student. She walked over to talk to a few of them standing in front of a sign masking taped to the table's front that said, "Save the Environment," a sign that she probably would have painted and taped to tables back in the day.

OPPOSITE DIRECTIONS

Sara's plan, if all went well with her meeting with President Adams, was to inform her company's board and her executive team that she was moving to Austin. Today's technology allows people to work from wherever they want. She had worked diligently to establish her firm's leadership team with tenure she could trust and be able to travel back and forth as needed. Sara decided that now, as a widow and successful business woman, she wanted to live in Austin, Texas, a place she fell in love with while a student. In other words, it was time for a life change.

TEN

DB Garcia is known throughout the office as a whiz in internet and social media research. It's not uncommon for others in the office to come to her to help them find information online. Sitting down to do a little research on Dennis Johnson should be a breeze. DB texts home to let her family know she will be leaving the office soon and will stop and pick up some pizza for dinner. A quick Google search, and then checking Facebook and Instagram, was enough to find the information on Bastrop County Commissioner Dennis T. Johnson that she needed for now.

Google links led to campaign stories and ads, speeches, and articles typical for what you expect to see for a county judge in Texas. Things like presiding over the Commissioner's Court, and handling county welfare and disaster relief issues. Multiple stories praised Dennis Johnson for handling the crisis management during a large forest fire that threatened the entire county and many homes of his constituents. In one article comparing him to an opponent running for County Judge, he is described as a native of Smithville, with much of his family still living there. It notes he is divorced with no children, notes some athletic achievement in high school, and that he received his college degree at Southwest Texas State University. There are also a couple of links to stories about a contested DUI in a neighboring county.

On social media, it seems he mostly forwards posts as opposed to creating any original posts. Most are about local county events and activities, and a few about sports and politics. Other than a few birthday wishes not much is personal and there is no mention or image of a red pick-up. Overall, a pretty clean, if not boring result from the searches. To DB, that was a good sign. But she knows some people are more careful to reveal themselves personally online, especially public officials. Finishing up her notes, she packs up her belongings and heads out to pick up pizza and then drive home.

ELEVEN

DB greets me with her 100-watt smile. She is holding a stack of papers.

"Welcome back, boss. You see what happens when you travel and are out of the office for longer than a week," she says laughing while following me into my office. "I'm sorry to get right to it after the week you just had and then having to deal with your sister's funeral on top of all that, but project deadlines are creating a little stress for our department heads," she demonstrates by holding up the stack of papers.

"No worries, DB", I assure her. "You have been with me through this long journey with Susan. We both know she is better off not suffering. Let's deal with this stack that you're holding. Plus, it will help take my mind off of all that."

After 45 minutes of going through all the requests, questions, and signing a couple of contracts, DB begins gathering up all her papers as I started to get ready for the day's first conference call.

"One last thing", DB said while standing to leave. "Here's what I found out about Dennis Johnson. There's not much. It seems he keeps his personal life off of social media as much as possible. The rest is just county judge campaign stories and ads, as well as some other county business."

I'm looking over her report. "Yeah, I still don't think he's much of a threat. He's an elected official, so it would be a serious threat to his career and livelihood for him to do something stupid. Although, I do see the DUI that Roger had mentioned. So, it's possible he's got a drinking problem. Let's just wait and see if anything else comes up. Thanks for checking, DB".

"Of course. I'll dig a little deeper when we have more time and see if I can find anything about a red pick-up truck, but for now I'll start getting these contracts and actions you just approved out to our department heads".

I make quick work of the days' calls and meetings. I purposely left the last few hours of the day open. Tonight is a big night. After a couple of close calls, I am finally in a relationship with someone that I am pretty sure is the one I will marry, Kelly. Tonight is the 2nd year anniversary of our first date. I need time to prepare because I want to make this a special night.

TWELVE

Kelly and I met at a mutual friend's wedding. We really hit it off over that weekend and decided to keep talking, eventually dating and spending more time with each other. Over these past two years we had traveled some together, but with my constant travel for business I was never the first one to suggest going somewhere for fun. She has always talked about traveling to Hawaii together and getting some nice and relaxing time on the beach. We both enjoy training together for triathlons, and just hanging around the condo watching Netflix on weekends. For me this is ideal since I travel so often for business. But, Kelly doesn't travel for work so she keeps nudging me to take time off and go somewhere—anywhere. Tonight, I am going to surprise her with tickets to Hawaii. But first, I needed to pick up some wine, some flowers, and her favorite dessert from the new French bakery that just opened in the neighborhood.

"Hey, sorry I missed you", I said as her voice mail picked up. "No worries. I'll see you this evening. Love ya!"

I've never had trouble meeting and dating smart, beautiful women. My problem is sustaining serious relationships. I know it's time for me to settle down with someone I can share my life with. In the past five years, I've seen two women that I loved move on with their lives, without me.

Jan had a hard time handling my travel schedule and me being gone all the time. She made a career change that moved her across the country, so felt it best that we end it as good friends. It was hard, but I understood.

Just a couple of years ago, Jill surprised me on Valentine's Day with a heartbreaking decision that she was not ready to settle down. She felt I was getting close to asking her to marry me, and she got a little scared. The truth is, I was shopping for a ring. After almost two years into the relationship, I had definitely misread her feelings for me. I loved my life, but I could feel time slipping away with no real plans to marry. I had chosen work over friends and the few friends I had were scattered across the country. They had their busy lives with work and family, and so I just poured myself more into my work.

Now with Kelly, I felt this was the time. I just had a good feeling about it. I thought a nice engagement would be a good next step to take in our relationship.

THIRTEEN

The condo is sparkling clean. Candles light the entry and the dining room table, surrounding the large centerpiece of freshly cut gladiolas in all colors. Dinner from our favorite Italian restaurant sits warming in the oven while the Oregon pinot noir is poured. Her favorite French dessert is chilling in the fridge as I wait for her to arrive home.

Knowing how much Kelly wants to go to Hawaii, I'm confident the plane tickets will be the highlight of the evening. I have been to Hawaii many times on business, but Kelly has never been. We constantly talk about going over together. Hawaii has been number one on her list for a while, and, of course, I love going to Hawaii whenever I get the chance. Up until now, we just haven't had the chance to go together because of our work schedules.

I have pictured this evening in my mind many times. She will come in tired from work and will be happy that a glass of wine is poured and dinner is prepared. We will have some wine, eat dinner, and over dessert I will casually ask her what her plans are for taking some time off work over the holidays. I know the conversation will eventually lead to our talking about how much fun it would be to go to Hawaii. I'll walk over to my desk, pick up an envelope and hand it to her. She'll quickly see that it's airline tickets and then see that Honolulu is the destination. It will be a big surprise and we will celebrate. I can't wait—it's going to be great.

FOURTEEN

My third call to Kelly goes unanswered. Again, direct to voice mail. Now I'm a little worried. Not about dinner in the oven but about her safety. I call her office and there is no answer there, either, just voice mail. Even though it's after hours, I leave a message asking her to call me because I'm getting worried about her. After another 30 minutes, I've been waiting long enough—something is not right. I go to get my car keys. My mind is now wandering and thinking she could have been in an accident. I'm going to go look for her. I reach for the door and my phone rings. It's her ringtone—Keith Urban's "Only You Can Love Me This Way".

"Hey."

Immediately, I can tell something is wrong by her voice. It's weak and uncertain. Normally it is upbeat and confident.

"Hey, I was getting worried. Are you okay?"

"I'm fine. I hate myself for doing this..." she began to cry.

"What...what do you mean? I ...I don't understand—why are you crying? Are you okay?" I reply as my heart begins to race.

I am really worried now and hoping she is not in any danger. "Just let me know where you are and I'll come and get you."

"No, this is hard for me. Stay where you are. I'm fine". And, then she began a tear-filled speech that, unfortunately, I've heard before. It's not you, it's me. You're great, I'm the one who is a terrible person. I'm sorry to do this by phone, but I just couldn't face you.

Even though it was familiar, it's not any easier to hear. My heart feels like it is in a vice being slowly squeezed tighter by each word that comes out of her mouth. My throat is dry and it's hard to swallow. I definitely can't talk. So, I listen, putting up no defense. The bottom is falling out of my world as her words continue. It's a slow-motion tumble deep into an abyss. Thoughts are bouncing around my mind.

What did I miss? Did I do something wrong? I was caught completely by surprise.

"I do love you. You are a great person, too good for me. I'm sorry to end it this way. I'll find a time when you are not around to stop by, get my things and drop off my key."

I still sit in silence on the other end. After a long pause, she continued.

"Well, aren't you even going to say anything?" she asked.

Taking a couple of deep breaths, I try to compose myself and say something. It doesn't work, I can't and just am not in the frame of mind to speak. I think about just hanging up, then think better of it.

"This is obviously a shock to me, a huge surprise." I finally blurt out and say good-bye. I hang up—numbly just staring at my phone.

The evening ended with a big surprise alright, just not the one I had planned.

Staring at the bottom of your glass
Hoping one day you'll make a dream last
But dreams come slow and they go so fast
You see her when you close your eyes
Maybe one day you'll understand why
Everything you touch surely dies...Passenger, Let Her Go

FIFTEEN

Sitting at the dining room table, staring at my empty glass, I reach for the bottle of wine. In the past, Susan has always helped me get through tough times, beginning with the loss of our parents. My sister and I have an everlasting connection, especially as the sole survivors of our family. I miss knowing that I can call her at times like this. We were always there for each other. Now she's gone and I'm feeling lost.

Each sip of wine, though, does begin to numb the pain. Before I know it, I'm staring at the bottom of a $100 bottle of Willamette Valley pinot from Alexana Vineyards. I spend the rest of the evening in deep reflection about my life and my lack of ability to find a lasting relationship. I wondered, as I seemed to do after the previous two relationships ended, if I would ever find the right person. That thought conjures up old memories. As the hours pass, a wine-enhanced theory tells me that thinking about what-ifs is a figment of time creating more meaningful memories that perhaps reality would reveal.

SIXTEEN

DB's regular call, my alarm, comes too early. After taking Kelly's gut punch last night, then healing my wounds with wine, I do not feel like facing the situation. I just want to sleep in. The phone just keeps ringing, so reluctantly I answer.

"Aloha, I hope y'all have already packed for your trip. How was your evening?", DB was trying to be so nice. She had no idea how terribly wrong last night had gone.

"Uh, hey DB. I overslept. Let me call you back," I said as I wanted to avoid this conversation before I had even had a cup of coffee.

"Well, okay sleepy head. I'll be here with the day's agenda waiting for your review".

Once DB hung up, I rolled to the side of the bed and slowly sat up. Waiting a few seconds for my head to clear, I got up and walked out to the kitchen, turned on the coffee pot, and then noticed that the dinner from last night was still in the oven. The 'warming dinner' was now a brown, burnt crisp ziti. Luckily it did not catch fire. However, it had left a mess. I'm really on a roll, I think to myself sarcastically. I open a window and the front door to let some fresh air in, and sitting on my doorstep is an envelope. It's early for a delivery, plus it's odd that it's on my door mat and not in my mailbox.

I pick up the envelope and there is nothing written on it. I open it and pull out a photo with a note that says, "You are not getting away with it this time!"

The photo is a selfie, taken by Susan, that shows her with Ben and Reggie on the hood of Ben's Olds 442. There is a date circled in red – August 30th – the date of the accident.

SEVENTEEN

It is time for me to face the music. Fighting rush hour traffic on the way to the office, I call DB.

"DB, it's me. I'm on my way in to the office and traffic is at a crawl. Let's cover some of items while I'm driving since I'm a little behind schedule. Maybe we can quickly get some things off the list." What I didn't tell her was that we have a lot more than just the agenda to talk about this morning.

DB is a true professional. She is dedicated and very serious about her career. It's what makes her one of the very best at what she does. On top of that, her loyalty and discretion has led to an undeniable trust between us and makes us an excellent team. I'm not sure what I'd do without her support. Over the years, these close bonds had made us good friends, as well. She knows my personal life, and I know about hers. She is always looking out for me, like inviting me to celebrate holidays with her family knowing I am single and will be alone. DB is a blessing—to me and to the success of our work.

The news about Kelly will crush her. She and Kelly have become friends. In a way this is also a break up for her. She will be shocked at how things turned out last night. But, when I tell her about the note I found this morning on the door step, feeling sorry about a breakup will pale in comparison.

After ticking through some items quickly, DB begins addressing the concerns our partners recently shared with the leadership team.

"DB, before we get too far into this item, let's pause and talk about it when I get to the office. I should be there in about 15 minutes". She was fine with that, although I sensed a little hesitancy in her voice since this was out of character for me to stop or pause before I made it into the parking lot. I made the decision that I need to tell DB the secret if I was going to ask her to help me.

DB, at this point, may be my closest friend. I know she will protect me from office gossip about Kelly. I've seen her shut down hushed talk in the hallways about my past failed relationships. It seems our staff love to talk about my personal life—"Mr. Unlucky in Love", the All-American guy that seemingly has it all, except for love. She will shield me the best she can, just like she always does.

And now, I will count on her even more once I reveal the secret Susan and I have guarded so closely all these years.

Turning up the volume, Lenny Kravitz' new song, "Here to Love", takes me the rest of the way through traffic and into the parking garage.

EIGHTEEN

After greeting our receptionist, I walk down the hall and into the executive wing. I find a note from DB on her desk saying she had to run down to talk briefly with our CFO. This gives me a little time to unpack my brief case and straighten out my desk. As I walked into my office, I noticed a large package from the McCombs School of Business, the nation's leading business school and my alma mater. I am grateful to be presented with the highest honor from the University, and grateful to Dean Smith for nominating me. I am proud of my school and have always let everyone know how important it was to me in the success I had achieved since graduating. To have my name among previous honorees like Texas oil billionaire 'Red' Rosen, computer magnate Mack Delaney, longtime U.S. Senator Dallas Jones and others is an honor and I am genuinely humbled by the gesture.

Seeing this package reminds me that I needed to call the dean, and since DB was still not back it is a good time to see if I can catch him. "Dean Smith, this is Frank", I began as he answered my call. "I'm calling to check in and to see if the President's Office is still okay with going forward with the award presentation. Have they said anything more about their investigation of the threatening voice mail?"

"Frank, good morning! It's good to hear from you. Yes, I spoke to someone in the President's Office yesterday and they are good to go. I was about to ask my assistant to call you and let you know". Dean Smith was always one of my biggest fans, and I was grateful knowing his support had helped ease the worries coming out of the administration team.

"Thanks so much for your support. I do appreciate it." I decided this morning not to tell him about the note left on my door until I had time to do some checking myself. No need to worry him or the administration again if this just turns out to be nothing.

I see that DB is back in her office. I walk across the lobby to let her know I'm off the phone and ready to meet. "DB, I just got off the phone with Dean Smith. I know you've made travel arrangements, but will you please make a note to add a day so I can drive down to work on Susan's estate. Come on into my office and let's continue the work we were doing earlier on the phone."

DB knows my personal situation as well as she does the business side. She knows the situation with my sister, and will make sure I have time to see Susan's attorney while I am in the area. As Susan's health continued to fade and her situation worsened, we had spent more time in hospice care than planned. Settling her estate, included paying these bills, as well as executing her last will and testament should not be too difficult after all the advanced planning this time gave us to complete. Smithville is only an hour's drive from Austin and the UT campus, and it's been a couple of weeks since I was there for the funeral. And, after the conversation we are about to have, DB may be joining me to check out more about the threats that seem to be coming from there.

NINETEEN

"DB, is there anything in that stack of papers you are holding that is urgent?"

"Well, it's all important, but I would say it's not urgent enough that we must handle right now. As long as we address it by the end of the day I think we'll be okay".

"Good, I need to talk to you about a couple of personal issues. First, about Kelly. It did not go quite like I thought it would last night."

"I could tell from your voice on our call this morning that something was up, so that's why I haven't brought it up yet. I am dying to hear, though, so what happened? Was she surprised and excited about the trip to Hawaii?"

"There was a surprise alright. But, the surprise was on me." As I went through each of the evening's events in detail—excruciating detail of the setting, the food, the flowers, the wine, and then the call—I could see DB shoulders drop and her cheeks began to glisten with flowing tears.

"I can't believe it! I thought I knew Kelly. This has just blindsided me."

"DB, me too."

I gave her a minute to process it, and honestly to also gather myself from getting too emotional, and then continued. "As hurt and surprised as I am, this is not the worst part of last night." I then explained how I found a note on the front porch that was left some time during the night. I showed DB the note and the photo. Her sadness immediately turned to alarm.

DB's first words were spoken softly. "Do you think it's from Dennis?"

"I do. I'm going to give you my Ring camera passcode so you can check and try and confirm this."

"Why this photo?" wondered DB. "I don't understand".

"DB, I really did not want to burden you with this, but there is a secret that Susan and I swore never to reveal. It was to remain a secret forever. Now, there is a chance that Dennis knows something he shouldn't. If he does, it could destroy some good people's reputations and possibly even cause their financial ruin."

DB was now noticeably intrigued.

"I trust you completely, you know, that right? I feel it is important that I bring you into this and ask for your help. I need to let you know the secret in hopes you can help me keep it a secret."

TWENTY

I began to share details with DB of the story and the secret that she would now guard, along with me, as threats to unveil it were becoming serious.

"Back in high school," I began as DB listened intently as I told the story, "Susan and I did not go out with friends. We did our best to stay focused on getting scholarships and didn't want anything to derail our efforts. One night, after literally three years of being disciplined to avoid it, we decided to risk it and go out. We kept it quiet, and since there was a big dance at the Fayette County Fairgrounds we knew just about everybody we knew would be out of town. I went with two buddies, Ben and Reggie. Susan just wanted to drive around. She took my car because her car was low on gas. We stuck to the country roads and we all had a laid-back evening driving the backroads and drinking a few cold beers. Then, as we were headed home for the night, the evening went sideways. Somehow, we think it was because she fell asleep, Susan wrecked my car into the town's beloved Rail Car Museum. She called me and Ben, Reggie and I raced to help her try and move the car out of the wreckage. She wasn't hurt, but the museum had my car in its lobby. Finally, after many attempts to move the car, I asked Ben and Reggie to take her home. It was getting too risky for someone to see us and I wanted to protect her, her reputation, and a scholarship she was scheduled to accept from the city in just a few short weeks.

After leaving the scene she asks Reggie and Ben not to take her home as I had asked them to do. She was too emotional, very worried about me, and just didn't want to be alone. Ben and Reggie, with Susan in the backseat, wound their way through the small-town streets making their way as inconspicuously as possible to see if they could catch a glimpse as to whether I had been successful in moving the car and leaving the scene before anyone noticed. When turning onto Main

Street's far end, away from the museum and railcar, their hearts sunk. Flashing red and blue lights. Police lights.

How could this happen to their buddy and brother, Frank. The guilt hit Reggie and Ben hard. The sorrow hit Susan just as hard. Each of them now regretted ever leaving me alone to deal with this, but it was what I had asked them to do.

Not sure what they could do, they asked Susan if they could drop her off at our house. She said no, deciding to ride along with them and try to comprehend what was going on. On the way out of town they stopped at the U-totem, grabbed another six pack, and hit the backroads. Susan sat pensively in the back seat staring out the car window. After a few more beers, and even more commiserating about the night's troubles, Susan fell asleep in the backseat.

Nobody will ever know for sure what happened next, but there is no doubt that too many beers led to a terrible accident. Ben and Reggie each drank a six-pack when with me, and then drank two to three more when driving with Susan. Their car took a turn going too fast on a one-lane backroad that had a mounded railroad crossing and was launched into the lake.

Susan was thrown out of the back window, hitting her head and stunned. Luckily, realizing she was sitting in shallow water, she somehow found her way to shore. She was in and out of consciousness, and after calling their names for what seemed like forever, she could not find the boys or the car. Thinking they must have left her, she started walking. Our house was only a couple miles from the lake and she was able to make it there even though still in a daze.

Getting home before dawn, Susan had come back to her senses after a couple of hours. She got cleaned up and headed down to the police station to see me and bail me out of jail. She would try to call Ben and Reggie once she knew the status on my situation and whether or not she could get me out of jail.

By mid-morning, she had me released and we then both began to hear from friends. It was tragic news—Ben and Reggie's wreck and drowning. In shock and inconsolable, both of us sat at home in silence for hours before committing to never tell anyone about the evening's events—thus "the secret" was born. Nobody knew Susan was even out since her car never left her house. I was in jail, so could not be tied to the accident. Ben and Reggie were good guys with great reputations around town. We felt that by remaining quiet and keeping this secret, the boys were assured hero funerals not tied to a night of drinking. Susan kept her reputation and scholarship, and I took the fall for the museum crash. I was arrested for vandalism but not for drinking and driving, a bit of luck if there was any in this entire situation. With hard work and a lot of humility, plus being good enough in sports to get me past a suspension from our athletic director and still gain a scholarship, the only lasting effect was going from local hero to a goat, a bum in the eyes of my hometown all because I was painted by the police as vandalizing the cherished Railcar and museum with damages and costs ranging in the thousands of dollars. Nobody believed it was an accident. It's a cross I bear today, so many years after all this and still a pariah in my own hometown, which I still love anyway despite it all

While having this heavy burden to carry did take its mental toll on both Susan and me, seeing Ben and Reggie's families settle with insurance for a life-changing $5 million, and seeing them memorialized as town heroes lifted some of that burden. Nothing could bring back our friends, but seeing them held in such high esteem did help ease some of the pain.

And, for me, watching as Susan built her prominent place in the town's leadership made the sacrifices worth it.

Now, with everyone gone except for me I was certain the secret would forever remain safe. I am somewhat stunned to hear that this old schoolmate had some piece of unknown evidence that threatens to unravel all this and potentially ruin the lives of Ben and Reggie's families, the reputations of my good friends, and my own professional standing and good reputation beyond the honor I will receive from the university. In my world, business success is built upon strong relationships. Nobody wants to be known as a liar. Nobody trusts a liar.

51

TWENTY-ONE

The last hour was a lot to take in, and both DB and I just sat in silence for a minute before I moved us back to work.

"Since the UT investigation shows there to be little to no threat from the voicemails, I am going to go ahead and go to Hawaii as planned. Well, not as planned. I'll go alone." I laughed nervously at this, but DB's expression remained solemn. "I need some time to digest all this, we can connect and handle any issues that are priority and then I still have time to work out, hike, and just relax on the beach in the afternoons and evenings.

DB agreed. "You need this trip. This is definitely a time that you need to take care of yourself." I'll do more research to see what I can find on our little note writer, just to make sure he is a harmless blowhard and drunk."

DB helped me rearrange my calendar, removing the plans I had made for Kelly and me, so I could spend a week on the glistening white sand beaches of Kailua and Lanikai on Oahu's windward side. With the 5-hour time difference, I will wake up early to do business on the mainland by phone and computer if needed, and then have all afternoon and evenings to relax.

My final words as she left my office were to thank her for being brought into my personal life and the secret she now would help keep. "DB, I appreciate, maybe more than I let you know, how much you support me—as an Executive Assistant, but just as much as my friend."

TWENTY-TWO

"In addition to posting all the information on your calendar so you have access to it on your phone, I also placed your travel itinerary on your desk. It includes some additional reading material that UT sent you about the award and the ceremony," DB informed me as I arrived back in the office after lunch.

"Thanks as always, DB. I plan to take off a little early this afternoon to go home and pack and get in a workout." She knows I always try to exercise before a long flight, so my leaving early for a workout was something DB had already planned on.

"I will email you our normal morning briefings. With the day-long flight and the time difference, I'll give you some time to adjust. And, Frank, use this time for you—enjoy it and try to relax if you can, even if it's just a little. I'll hold the fort down here."

TWENTY-THREE

I quickly make it through security and make my way to the gate. Traffic was worse than expected, so I only have a few minutes before boarding. I reach the gate and see there is a 30-minute delay. So, I walk over to grab a coffee where I see a young mother and her young daughter deep in discussion. I couldn't help but overhear their conversation.

"But Mommy, I have never been in an airplane before and now I have to fly over the whole ocean?! I want to go to Hawaii but I'm scared".

The young mother was soothing her and saying, "It will be okay. We will watch a movie and play games. The time will pass quickly."

"Excuse me," I said. "I apologize for interrupting. I couldn't help but overhear your conversation. I would like to do something for your daughter to help make sure her first flight is a good one. Are you okay with that?"

The mother was skeptical and questioned me, "What do you mean? What can you do to make sure her flight is a good one?"

I handed her my two boarding passes—mine and the one that was going to be Kelly's and was now my empty seat. "I'll trade you my two First Class tickets for yours and your daughter's tickets. I think she will find sitting up front will make her first flight a special one." If it wasn't going to be the special flight for me and Kelly that I had planned, maybe I could make it special for someone. And, who better than a sweet little girl and her mom?

I'm sure she thought I was nuts. But, after some reassurances from me she accepted. Forty-five minutes later, when I boarded the plane, I briefly looked up to the first-class cabin where I could see the young girl with a huge smile. She was already enjoying a cookie and some ice cream. I walked back to my seat, squeezed myself in and just hoped the person in front of me did not lean their seat back the entire flight.

TWENTY-FOUR

We arrived at Honolulu International Airport on time. I slept a few hours, did some work on the computer, and watched a movie. Even with all those distractions, the eight-hour flight is a long one. As I walked through the jetway and into the gate area, I see the mom and young daughter smiling from ear to ear. Being in first class, they had already been off the plane long enough to buy a lei and they presented it to me as a thank you. The little girl, who was also proudly wearing a lei, gave me a hug and told me it was the best flight and she couldn't wait to fly again.

After a quick stop at baggage claim, I made the short walk to the car rental area. There was no line in the premier lane, so I approached the counter without having to wait.

"Mr. Travis, your car is a new black Toyota Highlander and is number 3 in Row H. All the paperwork was done online, so here are the keys and we will see you in a week." And just like that, I was off. I smiled and thought to myself, thanks DB for making things so easy for me.

I drove from the airport on H1 toward Honolulu and then exited on Highway 61, the Pali Highway. Traffic on Oahu can be challenging at any time, but especially as the hospitality workers in the Waikiki hotels and resorts change shifts late in the afternoon. I plan to go into Waikiki later in the week, but I want to get to the Windward side of the island early enough to take a long afternoon swim in the ocean.

Even having made this drive many times, I am still in awe of the magnificent view that greets you—the lush Ko'olau mountain peak dropping steeply to the blue ocean and outlining the towns of Kaneohe and Kailua. I have reserved a house at Kai One Place in Kailua that includes a pool and a lawn that stretches all the way to the beach. With the windows down to enjoy this perfect Hawaiian day, I listen to the local 'Jawaiian' station on the car radio as I drive—a style of music blending Hawaiian sounds with Jamaican reggae. It is great to be back in Hawaii.

TWENTY-FIVE

The big red Ford pick-up pulls up in the alley behind Main Street offices and restaurants. Across the alley faces an automotive body shop. The rest is vacant lots used for parking at the funeral home across the street. Entering a backdoor, Dennis Johnson walks down the narrow hall of the historic building, past a small restroom and on to a larger work room and break room. Stacks of printer paper sit on top of the copier waiting to be put away. Grabbing a cup of coffee, he walks past a collage of photos from his high school days playing football and baseball and into the front lobby. His secretary, Tammy, looks at him, rolls her eyes at this habitual late arrival and nods a hello toward him. The lobby is modest having had only a few remodels over the years from its original state when built in 1895. With exposed brick and ductwork and lighting hanging from the high ceilings, it has a back-in-time feeling. Framed posters of the town's big Jamboree hang on the wall, along with photos with young Future Farmers of America students and their livestock that the office has sponsored over the years. Behind Tammy's desk is a Farmer's Almanac calendar, a signed movie poster from Hope Floats, a Hollywood movie that was filmed in town, and her desk and credenza is filled with pictures of her kids.

"Late again," Tammy says halfway under her breath.

"Leave me alone."

"We are not going to be able to afford to keep this office open if you don't start working again. I don't know what's gotten into you."

"Look, I'll take care of things." Pausing to take a long sip of coffee, Dennis continues, "I wanted to let you know that I just got a call from Billy over at the Constable's office. He asked me to do him a favor and serve a summons for him because he has to out of town. I owe him a favor, so I told him I would do it. You should see a check from him coming in the mail."

This calmed Tammy a little. She was happy to know some income was on the way and would cover some of the invoices sitting on her desk. Dennis walked back to his office, sat down, and stared at an old photo from his high school days. A smile slowly appeared as he thought about how he would get his revenge in a couple of days.

TWENTY-SIX

"Good morning everyone! How is everyone doing today?" Sara always made an upbeat, positive entrance to her Monday morning staff meetings with her executive team. It was a good way to chase away any Monday blues and to get the week off to a good start.

Her team, all standing near the coffee and bagels, begins to find their seats as Sara grabs her own cup of coffee. The Board room is in the CEO Suite and is where all the Monday meetings are held. Typical of many law firm's offices, its walls are covered in dark wood paneling, large pieces of framed art from around the world hang strategically around the room, and the floor to ceiling windows have shades that can be drawn when needed by remote control. But, today there will be no Power Point slides and no need to close the room off from the brilliant blue sky as they gaze out over the city from the 35th floor.

Sitting down at the head of the table, the firm's internal legal counsel Tom is to her right. Kelsey, a public policy specialist, is seated next to him, and Chris, who leads HR, is across the table next to Randal, who leads the new business group.

Chris asked, "Sorry to ask so late, but I didn't get an agenda for this morning. Can someone post it to our intranet so I can grab it real fast?"

"There is no written agenda for this morning. I have only one topic for us", Sara begins as she addresses the entire team.

"This is something that has taken much of my time and energy as I've carefully considered over the past months. You all know that I've been asked to serve on the University of Texas' President's Council and will be going to Austin to meet with the president and hear more about this role. While I'm there, I have set up an appointment with a real estate agent to look for a home."

There was initially silence, before Kelsey asked, "So you are looking for a second home in Austin?"

"No, I plan to sell my home here and move there. I know you are going to have a lot of questions, and we will stay here until I answer them. I assure you that I am not leaving the firm. I don't plan on any major changes, other than I will work remotely and telecommute when necessary. "

Sara then spent the rest of the morning answering questions from her team and talking about the new way of work with her being remote. She asked them not to say anything yet, as she would personally let the clients and staff here it from her. She trusted this group to lead, as they already did with each of them representing a part of the firm and its 600 attorneys and support staff.

Leaving the office that afternoon, Sara felt a little uneasy and a little excited about the upcoming change. She hated to leave the home she had built with her husband, and while she would be leaving it, she knew that she would not leave him and his memories in a building—they would always be with her. But, after seven years, she was open to finding someone that she could share life with—ups and downs, she realized, were best shared with a spouse. Having gone on a few dates over the past year, it reminded her how nice it was to have someone care about your day, your challenges and successes. She had mourned, and would always have a deep love for her late husband, but felt she had so much more life to live. A new start in a new place was what she felt was needed.

TWENTY-SEVEN

Driving into Kailua, I stop at Food Land to stock up on snacks and drinks on the way to the beach house rental. I arrive at the beach house, unload the bags from the car and just put away the things that need to be refrigerated. I'll unpack everything when I get back. I change quickly into my running and swimming gear and head out the back door for a run on the beach and then a swim—once up the beach to Kalama park and then down to Kailua Beach Park. After a short stint at Kailua Beach Park, I continue and walk down the beach to my favorite spot, Lanikai beach. It is a little more secluded and is the place where I feel a calm come over me. Today would just be a quick visit knowing I would spend much more time here in the coming days.

On the walk back, I stop at Buzz's Steakhouse, a small, non-descript restaurant that looks more like a dive than a steakhouse. In business since 1962, its popular with the locals and those who park across the street at the park. All the food is excellent, but I was there to enjoy a drink at the bar before walking the rest of the way back to the beach house rental.

My runs, swims and walks are where I have some serious conversations with myself. The exercise, along with the soothing environment of one of the most beautiful places on earth, allows me to dig deep into self-evaluation while keeping in shape for the upcoming triathlon. My first night at Buzz's, I sit alone and quietly sip a very strong Mai Tai with its deep pool of rum floating on top. There are some early diners and a few others at the far end of the bar. After a quiet and relaxing drink, I am headed out as a line has formed outside with people waiting to be seated. Walking back at dusk along the beach, the waves gently kiss the sandy shore, rolling across my feet in hushed tones that provide the perfect ending to my day.

TWENTY-EIGHT

Time always seems to pass too quickly when I am in Hawaii. This time is no different. I wake up at 3 am local time, which is 8 am back at the office. It's time to grab a cup of coffee and catch up on email. I know DB will only engage me with the mainland business activity when absolutely necessary, which unfortunately includes the issue with Dennis and his threats. After getting in my run and swim, the rest of the day I will fill with hiking, and a walk on the beach. No calls today. Just a lot of emails and texts. It gives me time to draft some remarks for the upcoming awards ceremony. After a few hours, I text DB an "all ok" and she responds with an "all okay here." Work is done for today.

Today I will hike the Ka'iwa Ridge Trail, better known as the Pillbox Trail. It's not too difficult but is a good workout with great views along the 2-mile trail. Because it's steep and narrow in many places, it takes about an hour unless, like me, you sit at the top and admire the amazing views of Lanikai and Kailua and the amazing beaches and aqua blue water along the shoreline. I spend a good amount of time in thought, while every once in a while talking to other hikers who share the amazing view. There's plenty to like about this hike, and one thing is that on the way back down the trail, you can easily walk over to Lanikai beach to swim and cool off—which of course I do.

TWENTY-NINE

After being in Hawaii a couple of days I am able to totally relax while hanging out on the Windward side of Oahu. The ocean, the beaches, the gentle trade winds blowing off the cool Pacific water have a way of doing that.

Today, hours before the sun would rise, I was out on the beach. I stood for a while gazing at the bright stars filling the dark sky. Then, I begin casually strolling along the moonlit beach with stars reflecting like glitter against a calm sea, stopping a few times to just sit in the sand and listen to the soothing surf rolling onto the shore and then back out. I reach Lanikai beach just about the time when the night becomes the morning. Sitting on the sugary white sand, the stars begin to fade and the horizon takes on a soft orange glow of a million burning embers. I am ready to reflect on the last conversation I had with Susan.

My last conversation with Susan should have made an immediate impact on me. Avoiding the process of grieving for her had prevented me from understanding what she was telling me. But, even so, I did remember just about every word.

Susan and I had always been close. After losing our parents, we became each other's best friend. We confided in each other, trusted each other implicitly, and kept each other humble and honest.

I could not stop thinking about the different paths our lives had taken from our small, rural central Texas town.

A scholarship allowed me to attend the University of Texas and created so many opportunities that I was able to take advantage of with great success. Susan's scholarship gave her many opportunities and she was happy and successful on her own terms in becoming a leader in the town she loved. Then came the diagnosis of ALS. Living her entire life in our hometown, her friends became a family of support and helped take care of her for years as the disease eventually incapacitated her. True friends that shared her life. That was something I did not have.

My friends were from my business relationships. These were treasured friendships with great people, but it wasn't the same as lifelong friends. I was losing my best friend to ALS. I considered DB to be a close friend, but of course she had her family and friends and I couldn't allow her to take her time and attention away from them any more than I already caused her to do through our work together.

With the ALS robbing her of the ability to speak, Susan's words were strained and halting, but we were patient. It broke my heart to see how quickly the disease was choking off her words. It was unsaid between us, but we both knew this could be our last time to actually talk, so we took all the time that was needed.

We covered a lot of ground, many things we had not spoken of in years but were huge impacts on our lives. As difficult as it was, we talked about the tragedy that took our parents. For so many years, we had tried our best not to think about it. We wanted it out of our minds. But, we needed to talk about it now.

THIRTY

We were in our mid-teens. Our mom and dad were great parents, sacrificing so much to support our wants and needs growing up. They put us first, and their personal lives second. After years, we were finally at a point to where they could leave us home alone and go out on date nights. They usually ate an early dinner so they could catch a movie early enough and make it back home before 10 pm. One night it was 10:30 and they had not yet made it home. Susan and I thought it was odd, but we weren't overly worried. Then when it was 11 pm and they still weren't home we began to worry. Not long after 11, the doorbell rang. Standing outside the front door was a Texas Highway patrol officer. Susan and I were both at the door when we opened it. Before the officer could finish introducing herself, we saw my Aunt hurriedly walking over from her house next door. We all knew something was not right. It's not normal for the Texas Highway patrol to visit people in their homes.

As soon as we heard the officer say, "I'm sorry to inform you that your parents were in an accident..." everything just went silent and we grabbed onto each other and began to sob. Luckily, my Aunt was right there for us. I know as hard as it was on us, it was just as hard on her to hear she had lost her sister and favorite brother-in-law, but she held it together for us.

That night was truly a nightmare. And, it was a nightmare we wanted to forget. After grieving for months, and learning the details that caused the accident—a deer jumping onto the road in front of a car traveling the opposite direction and causing that car to cross the highway and directly into my parents—we knew that it was the fault of no one and just a terrible case of being in the wrong place at the wrong time. For Susan and I, time eventually helped to heal. But it was a slow process and we depended on each other to pick the other up when one of us began to feel down.

Because of our ages, and the fact that our Aunt lived next door, we were able to remain living in the house while eating our meals and spending quite a bit of time next door with our Aunt. Technically we lived with our Aunt, but realistically we stayed next door in our home most of the time.

We also spoke about the secret we had kept between us. Both of us were in tears as we remembered Ben and Reggie and relived that terrible night. The guilt we had about the whole situation was overshadowed by the town's respect in memorializing them and by their brothers and sisters benefiting from the insurance settlement.

That day, we talked for hours. We covered our time growing up together, and our time separated as I left our hometown for college and never moved back home. We talked often by phone, but there were times I only made it back home to visit once or twice a year. We remained close—best friends—in spite of not seeing each other often but always staying in contact. We talked about our different paths in life, and how each of us chose what was right for us. Our final topic, before Susan was just too tired to go on, was about relationships. Susan was worried about me. She asked me, as only she could, about my past failed relationships and what my future plans may be. But it hit me hardest when, faced with the stark reality of what was to come with her disease's progression, she told me she was concerned about what I would do once she was gone. We both had tears in our eyes, both understanding that when she was gone I would need someone I could share my life with and rely on, as I had relied on Susan, to confide in.

Susan was at peace knowing what was ahead for her. She wanted to be at peace knowing that I was going to be okay when she was gone.

THIRTY-ONE

When I returned to the beach house I thought about just sitting out on the lanai and nursing a cold beer. But, I decided to walk along the beach as the sun was setting and ended up back at Buzz's. Tonight, the bar was full and the only available seat was at the end of the bar next to an older, elegant woman. She was obviously a local, as everyone seemed to either stop and say hello or wave to her from across the room.

I introduced myself. "Hi, I'm Frank."

She looked at me, paused just enough to make me wonder if she had heard me, and then smiled. "Hi Frank. I'm Jenny".

Striking up a conversation with her I found that she was waiting on her daughter, who was stuck in Honolulu traffic and running late.

I saw that she was drinking a vodka, so ordered her another and the same for me. Lost in conversation, and two more drinks later, she looked at me and said, "Frank, thanks for sharing your story with me. I've got a few stories for you, too. But, let's let them wait for another day."

I'm not sure why I opened up and told a complete stranger my woes. It may have been due in part to the vodka. But it was also her—she was calm, wise, and experienced in life. I did let her talk enough to learn that she had been an eyewitness to the bombing of Pearl Harbor. She is a leading advocate in the women's rights movement, and earlier in life had been an active supporter of civil rights advances in Hawaii. She looked so young to have lived a full and interesting Forest Gump-like life. I took her words as the trusted advice of a new and wise friend.

"Frank, first of all, it is okay to grieve for your sister. You need to do this so that you can release her as being your best friend and confidant. It's time you find your happiness and someone with whom you want to share your life. But, most importantly, I tell you this from experience, it's not always about what's *next*. It's about what's *now*. These words may sound cliché, but follow your heart. Don't be afraid of making a mistake. Act for yourself—be present."

A beautiful young woman suddenly taps her on her shoulder, interrupting us. "Hi, Mom. Sorry it took so long." I could see so much of her in her daughter's face, and the spunk in her spirit as she put her arm around Jenny and they were off to a dinner for which they were very late.

She didn't say it, but the message was clear to me. I need to meet Dennis face to face and act on whatever this was that was driving him to act this way.

Walking back to the beach house, I recognized how powerful those words were—"it's not always about what's next." That was how I succeeded my entire career. Moving forward, being bold and unafraid, being the first and continuing to stay ahead of my competition. It's about what's now—I was not enjoying the fruits of my hard work and success. I was not being present in my relationships. No matter how much I tried, a true relationship is a partnership and I needed to be present. I needed to be me, not just try to please the women in my life and do what I thought they wanted. I needed to be me, authentically.

THIRTY-TWO

I am calm. My mind is clear. I approach the beach house with Jenny's words echoing in my mind. A notification on my phone breaks the silent night. A text appears from DB. "Red truck confirmed to be Dennis Johnson." It would be the last day at the beach house, and last day in Hawaii. It is imperative I return.

THIRTY-THREE

I fumble for the key, unlock the back door to the beach house and step inside and immediately call DB.

"Aloha, DB, how are things back on the mainland?"

"Hey, it's good to hear from you Frank. Sorry to interrupt your Hawaii trip with that text message," replied DB. "I'll give you all the details on my research of Dennis, there's more than the red truck."

"I'm guessing that the Ring camera shows that he was the one leaving the message and photo on my front door step. I'll be coming back as soon as you can arrange a flight for me."

I anticipated you would want to come back early, I have all the information loaded on the airline's website and all I have to do is to hit enter and you'll be on the red eye."

"Thanks for working last minute with the airline to get me back right away. I plan to come straight from the airport to the office when I arrive in the morning."

I was taking the red-eye flight that left Honolulu at 10 pm local time and would get me back home around 10:30 am.

"And, by the way, the University of Texas staff have sent all the details for the meeting and your award presentation. I'll pull all that together for you and meet you at the office in the morning".

DB was so organized, that I didn't even feel any anxiety about returning from a time away. I knew she had things under control.

THIRTY-FOUR

I poured the last bit of Pinot from the bottle and walked outside one last time to the lanai to sit back and think about these past few days. The trade winds were calm but cool, and the night sky was filled with a million stars. Moonlight reflected off the surf as it hit the sandy shoreline. This is as relaxed as I've been in a while, even knowing I've got to pack quickly to head back and knowing what awaits me at home. I can't stop thinking about the conversation I had earlier with the kind woman in the bar. I've never shared like that, even with people I've known for a long time. Her words hit me squarely in the chest and I realized that I have been avoiding too many things in my life. It's not been fair to others, but especially to myself. I made up my mind, I would deal with Dennis directly. I would not put it off on someone or something else—DB, the UT investigators, or internet searches. After the UT event, I would use my extra day in Smithville to find Dennis and end this nonsense.

THIRTY-FIVE

Jet lag always gets me the first few days back from Hawaii. Some of this is truly jet lag, and some is just me trying to hold onto as much aloha as I can before I fall back into my daily routines. I will definitely be taking some of that aloha spirit with me to the UT awards ceremony, but driving to Smithville to face Dennis, aloha doesn't stand a chance of lasting that long.

We land on time and I make it through baggage claim, to my car, and drive directly to the office to meet DB. I only have a few hours before boarding another plane to fly to Austin, we have to get to the bottom of this ridiculous behavior and the nuisance of these threats from a guy I knew years ago and haven't seen or talked to in decades. And, most importantly, I have to protect the secret that he now seems to have some knowledge about.

THIRTY-SIX

Sara is standing in line to board her plane to Austin when her cell phone rings.

"Ms. Cousins, this is Lisa from the president's office. We got your message about not receiving the pre-meeting reading and the agenda. We checked and found it was mailed to the wrong address. We are so sorry and want to apologize." Sara could tell the young woman of the phone was noticeably nervous, so she tried to put her at ease.

"Thank you for calling me back. Our flight was delayed, so I'm boarding a plane now. Would you mind bringing the information to the breakfast meeting in the morning and I'll review it before the council meeting begins." As one of the new council members, Sara really wanted to be prepared as well as possible, but she would just have to dive in quickly before the council meeting tomorrow. In her line of work, being a quick study was second nature.

"I can do better than that, Ms. Cousins. It will all be waiting for you at the hotel front desk when you check in."

THIRTY-SEVEN

I arrived at Austin Bergstrom International Airport a day early for the award ceremony. The early morning flight was the most convenient flight DB could find. I would spend the day working from my hotel room. The Driskill Hotel was quiet with only a few people scattered around the lobby when I walk in. With the renowned and impeccable customer service the hotel is known for, I am able to get into my room early with no problem. I get through the work I need to and make a call to an old friend I had recently been in touch with regarding the threats I was receiving.

"Chris, it's Frank. I made it in and would love to get some dinner and see a show at Stubbs if you are still up for it?" Frank knew he needed to confirm the evening's plans before it got too late. Chris confirmed that the plan was still on, and told Frank he would pick him up around 8 pm. He also mentioned that he had the report that Frank had asked for, and would bring it along so they could discuss.

Chris is a former colleague from our McKay consulting days. It will be good to catch up with him after not seeing him for many years. His career, after years of consulting work, took a huge turn and he is now one of Austin's best-known private investigators.

"Sounds great, Chris. That's a little later than I normally go to dinner, but I know live music doesn't really get going until about 10:00 pm. I'll meet you in the lobby of the Driskill. I'll buy you a drink and we can talk about what you've been able to discover. See you in a few hours."

I hung up the phone and texted DB to make sure work was done and there was nothing else needed from me today. I changed and went for run and then once back and showered I spent time reviewing the information for tomorrow's ceremony.

THIRTY-EIGHT

Pulling the letter from its envelope, I read through the information. The award would be announced before the lunch. I would have 10-15 minutes to address the group. It would be a small group of 125, and include the other council members and their spouses, the University Chancellor and her leadership team, Deans from all the schools and a few local government officials. Three new appointees to the council will also be recognized.

It's a big deal when new members to the President's Council are appointed. They tend to be the cream of the crop. The letter listed each new member, followed by a brief summary about them.

Sean Hill, a graduate of the College of Communications and the Chief Technology Officer of the world's largest social media network, Facebook. Glenda Williams, former State Attorney General and current CEO of Diversity One, a human resources firm. The third new board member was Sara Cousins, a renowned attorney with an impressive record of serving a Supreme Court Justice, being the first woman to be a managing partner in MM&N, the largest law firm in the US, and now CEO of her own company that had grown into a global firm with locations in seven countries and most of the major US cities.

It was an impressive list. I did not know any of them from my time as a student or my work with the University. I looked forward to meeting them.

THIRTY-NINE

Sara left her suitcase with the Bell Captain and approached the desk. Recently renovated, the Driskill Hotel is an iconic and historic hotel in downtown Austin. The renovations have not changed the atmosphere and grandeur of the famous old hotel. Stone columns stretch 30 feet upwards from the ornate marble tile floor to the 18th century stained glass-covered ceiling. Tall green palms line the path to the front desk, and in the distance frames a magnificent grand old staircase. Stepping into the lobby immediately transforms you from modern day to the classic splendor of a place where the elite Texas cattle barons gathered when coming to the capitol city.

"Welcome to the Driskill Hotel, Ms. Cousins. We are sorry your flight was delayed and hope you are able to get settled in right away. Your room is waiting and here's a package that was left for you with instructions to make sure we got this to you right away. Arthur will show you to your room and bring your bags." Sara traveled frequently and was used to good service, but she knew the President must have had something to do with this as they were waiting for her and didn't even ask for ID or a credit card for incidentals as is customary for all hotel guests.

"Thank you very much. I appreciate your help," she replied and turned to follow the bellman, Arthur, to her room. The lobby was bustling with people, so Arthur began to slowly weave his way across the lobby and to the bank of elevators.

FORTY

"We should probably make our way over to the Roaring Fork. Our reservation is for 8:30 pm," Chris said as he stood up from the bar stool. I paid for our drinks and followed Chris as he moved carefully through the crowded lobby. My mind is still processing Chris' report when he suddenly moved to his left. I keep going straight and literally bump into a woman who is looking down at her phone and doesn't see me.

"Excuse me!" I said as she looked up. Both startled, we freeze for a second.

"Sara?"

"Frank?"

"What a surprise," I said. "It is so great to see you after all these years. You look great."

"Well, it's definitely a surprise to bump into you," she said as we laughed at her attempt at humor. "Are you in Austin for long?"

"Just a couple of days. How about you?"

As we were attempting to catch up, Chris had made his way back to get me. He was insistent that we had to leave now of we would miss the dinner reservation. The bellman had continued walking, leaving Sara behind. She kept looking anxiously over her shoulder to find him through the crowd and her suitcase that he was carrying.

We both laughed, "Here we are, going in opposite directions again".

"Let's try to connect tomorrow, I'll leave you a note at the desk with my contact information," I said as Chris was now literally pulling on my jacket.

"I'll be out at a meeting most of the day tomorrow," said Sara. "It's great to see you. I hope we can connect. It would be so nice to catch up".

After walking out the hotel's front door, I began to regain my senses from the shock of running into Sara. This was a person that I couldn't get out of my thoughts over all these years. What were the odds that we would meet like this? I was not going to chance missing an opportunity to catch up with her.

"Chris, give me a minute," I didn't want to seem rude, so I quickly explained the situation to him and asked him to go ahead and let me meet him at the restaurant. As Chris walked up the block to the Roaring Fork, I went back inside to the elevator bank but she was gone. I went immediately to the desk and asked for Sara Ross.

"There is no Sara Ross registered," reports the hotel staff member who is still looking at her computer screen.

"No, I just saw her in the lobby and she said she is registered and staying here." I asked them to check again. But, after checking again I got the same answer. All I could imagine is that she was now married and registered under her married name. I told her I'd leave my contact information at the desk, now I had no idea how to leave it for her to contact me. Had I missed her?! Again?

I walked to the Roaring Fork and ate a great steak but could not enjoy it. I was a poor excuse for a friend to Chris as I was bummed out the rest of the evening. First, the report on Dennis and now this missed connection with Sara. What was I thinking to leave her again without at least exchanging our contact information? It seemed like deja` vu.

FORTY-ONE

Sara was up early. The President's office had a car waiting to take her to her breakfast meeting. She had one stop to make before walking over to the waiting car and heading over to campus.

"Will you please check and see if I have a message?" Sara asked the young man at the front desk. She was certain Frank had left his contact information. She had felt a sincere reconnect, just in the brief moment, and had hardly slept all night after remembering the feelings she had for Frank and had to forget as he graduated and moved away to begin a career so many years ago. She kept thinking that she should have stayed to talk with him in the lobby and not run off in search of the bellman and her bag.

"No ma'am, there are not messages for you."

"Are you certain? Can you please double check," Sara replied as she suddenly felt a little twinge in her stomach. Why wouldn't he have left her a way to contact him?

After waiting a few more minutes and having no messages found, Sara didn't want the driver to wait any longer. Distracted as she drove away from the hotel and down Congress Avenue towards the UT campus, Sara had to put her emotions aside and try to concentrate on the work at hand. This was her first meeting as a member of the President's Council and she was determined to make a good first impression.

FORTY-TWO

I was up early, but really had not slept much at all. I couldn't stop thinking about Sara. While the meeting and award presentation did not start until 10:30 am, I was dressed and ready and in the lobby by 7 am. Surely, I would catch Sara as she was on her way to breakfast or checking out. By 9 am it was clear that I may have missed her again. I would have to leave soon to make it to campus, check in with Dean Smith, and then head over to the conference center where the President's Council was meeting. On a day that should be such a happy occasion, I felt a fog of sadness setting in. Vowing to tackle the mystery of Sara's last name or whereabouts after the awards ceremony, I gave myself a personal pep talk on my drive to campus and by the time I arrived, I was ready to enjoy the next few hours and show my deep respect and appreciation for those who were making this recognition possible. Lurking in the back of my mind was concern about whether or not Dennis would make good on his threat.

FORTY-THREE

The President's breakfast was held in the ornate old Main Building, one floor below the President's Office. The room was set around a massive Texas oak conference table, with catering staff covering each corner of the room ready to serve council members and staff efficiently, but elegantly. Sara made her way around the room with purpose, introducing herself to each of the council members. Having missed last evening's dinner, she did not have the same opportunity as others to get to know each other. President Adams' chief of staff announced the breakfast meeting would begin in five minutes and asked everyone to begin taking their seat around the massive table adorned with several centerpieces of yellow roses mixed with the Texas state flower, bluebonnets. As breakfast was served, the staff made sure Sara had received the meeting packet and agenda that was shared with the others at dinner the night before.

"We will do a final review of the agenda while we have breakfast this morning, if that is okay with everyone," said President Adams. "There are a few additions and changes. If you have any questions, we will do our best to answer them. Then, we can enjoy our meal and begin walking over to the conference center for the meeting. Today's meeting begins at 10:30, so you'll have an hour or so to make your way over."

Sara opened her packet and pulled out the agenda. She would take time to review all the documents and background materials during the hour break. As she followed along, President Adams came to the place on the agenda where they would recognize one of their top alums with the President's Award.

"We are very happy that this year's honoree is Frank Travis, whom I know many of you know. He has had a very successful career and has proudly represented the University with dignity and honor since his graduation from the McCombs School of Business".

President Adams continued to speak, but Sara no longer heard his words. A mixed feeling of surprise and excitement, and a little trepidation that came over her. It was wonderful to know she would be seeing Frank again in a couple of hours. She was very happy to see that he would receive this great honor. But, she still wondered why he had not left her his contact information at the front desk. Maybe she was reading too much into it. She had important work to do as a member of the President's Council and was determined not to let this distract her. But, it was not going to be an easy task.

The agenda review went quickly. Breakfast was spent sitting next to one of the President's staff who updated Sara on the previous evening's activities. After breakfast ended and the small talk between council members subsided, Sara was shown to a small, quiet office upstairs in the President's suite where she spent the next 30 minutes studying the meeting packet information. With 15 minutes before the meeting was to begin, Sara gathered her things to make the short walk to the conference center for the meeting.

FORTY-FOUR

"Frank, thanks for spending some time this morning with us here at McCombs," said Dean Smith. "Our faculty members really appreciate the opportunity to spend time with you, and since they don't attend the President's Council meetings, they were afraid they may not be able to congratulate you personally."

"It's my pleasure, Dean," I replied. "I am humbled by the honor, and also by their kind words to me. I truly respect the work that you are all are doing that keeps advancing the ranking and status of the School."

The walk to the meeting site was short, but to Frank, any walk around the campus was a beautiful walk. It was a perfect 75-degrees with only a hint of humidity. The bright blue sky was absent of clouds. Exiting the McCombs Business School, they face the Perry-Castaneda Library and its brutalist architecture, a style that makes use of exposed, unpainted concrete and bricks and predominantly monochrome in color. As they walk up the hill, the Littlefield Fountain is in full display with its water fountains shooting over the huge pools and framing the stampeding horse sculptures splashing in the water. The University Tower frames the Texas-sized background. Crossing the street and seeing the majestic Texas State Capitol as they near the conference center makes this short walk as pleasant as any on campus.

FORTY-FIVE

I have never attended a President's Council meeting, but Dean Smith prepared me with regard to the traditions in pomp and circumstance and protocols to be observed. All guests and staff enter first and find seating in a gallery that covers the back third of the conference room. I am seated at a table reserved for special guests. In addition to me, it includes a couple of guest speakers. One is scheduled to provide a forecast on the Texas economy for the council, and the other special guests are two principles of an ad agency the council had hired to develop a campaign for the University system. They will all be participating in today's meeting and seem to be preoccupied with their presentations, so after introductions and small talk, I begin to read through the agenda while waiting for the council members to arrive and be seated.

After a few minutes, the gallery is asked to stand. The President's Council is announced and its members enter single file through a side door, led by President Adams. It reminds me of a graduation ceremony. One by one, they walk in single file and to their places that are marked by table signs made of Texas live oak with their names etched in bold lettering.

I cannot believe my eyes as the final council member enters the room. It's Sara. I am both excited and stunned at the same time, and totally distracted now by the thought that I need to speak to her as soon as there is a break in the meeting. I watch carefully as Sara walks around the room to a seat at the table with the name Sara Cousins. That is it. That is why I couldn't find her registered at the hotel. She is obviously married and with a different name now. My excitement remains, but now there is a bit of a letdown. Maybe I am reading too much into the brief encounter last night and she was just happy in seeing an old friend.

During the meeting, I can't keep my eyes off of her. Sara seems to be so focused on the meeting, that I am not sure that she has seen me in the audience. But, she must know that I'm here since my name is on the agenda to receive the award. Finally, I catch her glancing over and our eyes connect. We both smile.

From the budget conversation to the comments on the economic forecasts, the scope and depth of Sara's understanding and poise among this group and these conversations is impressive. Each time she has the floor, whether it is a question or a comment, she holds the entire room with her measured tone and obvious knowledge of the subject. This is not the same smart and beautiful girl I knew from years ago, but an even smarter and more beautiful woman. I am happy to see her and to see how successful she has become.

Now it's my turn, and I see that she is definitely looking now as I am being introduced. Still distracted, I work to focus on the next 10 minutes while being honored. After a short video tribute, I rise to walk forward to the podium. As I do, the council members and the entire room rise in applause.

FORTY-SIX

After my acceptance speech and the standard 'grip and grin' photos with the President and the council's chair, a 15-minute break is announced. My first instinct is to find Sara. However, what I failed to realize is that all the council members, staff, and some guests would come forward and be lined up and waiting to greet me and congratulate me personally. Of course, this is so generous and I do appreciate each and everyone's personal note of congratulations despite my eagerness to speak with Sara. I find myself, in between thanking them for their kind words and waiting for the next person to move forward, scanning the room looking for Sara. She is not in line to greet me, but is huddled in a corner with two other council members, most likely discussing an upcoming issue the council will address.

The line finally dwindles to a few. That's when I see Sara walking my way. Without being rude, I hurriedly speak with the final people in line and come to the last one—Sara. We both smile.

"Congratulations, Frank. What a wonderful honor for you to receive," Sara said holding out her hand to shake mine. "I had no idea of how your career took off and of all the wonderful things you've been able to do in business and for the University."

"Sara, thanks. Congratulations to you! A member of the President's Council, now that is really quite an honor." I replied. "I have to tell you how stupid I felt last night just assuming your last name was still Ross. When I went to leave you my contact information, the front desk could not find you registered. I thought I may have missed you."

Sara took this all in, not reacting in any way other than being professional. So, she thought to herself, he had tried to leave me a note at the desk. Not knowing my married name is an honest mistake.

The conference center meeting staff began ringing the chimes indicating it was time for everyone to take their seats and the meeting to re-start.

"Well, I need to take my seat," Sara interrupted. "I hope you are not leaving right away and will have some time after the meeting for coffee or a drink so we can at least catch up a little."

"By all means, let's do that," Frank answered without hesitation. "I'll meet you in the conference center's restaurant. I'll make a 4:30 reservation during the lunch break. Your meeting ends at 4, so that should give you enough time so you are not rushed. Should I make it for two, or is there anyone else I need to include?"

"No, just me", Sara said casually as she turned to walk to her seat to continue the meeting.

Since first seeing Sara last night, my emotions have bounced around from surprised to excited, curious, worried, tentative, happy, and impatient, all within the last 12 hours. It's like I'm some high schooler with a school boy crush. It is, however, making me realize how hard it was to break off our relationship when I graduated and left UT, Austin, and Sara behind.

I stay in the meeting through lunch, eating at the President's table with the special guests, and then excused myself as soon as it was clear that the President was finished as he was called away by one of the staff members.

Dean Smith joined me and we walked out of the conference center together.

"Dean, I can't thank you and your staff enough. This has really been a special day for me". Before I could continue, Dean Smith interjected.

"Frank, our thanks go to you. You have deserved this honor for some time, I know you think it's because you have given us money, and while there is probably some truth in that I want you to know that truly those monetary gifts are secondary to your gifts of time and leadership, and the halo your prestigious work brings to our business school and to this University."

"You're a good man, Dean. And, a good friend. I am touched. I will not forget this day," I said as we approached the doors leading outside and parted ways. He was off to his office, and I had a stop to make at the conference center's restaurant.

FORTY-SEVEN

Looking at my phone for the first time since the meeting had begun, I notice a text message I missed about 30 minutes ago. It read, "Tracker that Chris placed on red truck shows that he is in Austin and only blocks away from campus. Call me!"

I call DB immediately. "Your text came when I was with the President, so I had notifications turned off. I just saw it. What's the status now?"

"Well, like most things related to Dennis' actions, it's weird." DB went on to explain that the tracking device had shown Dennis on campus near the conference center, but only for about 5 minutes. Then, again, it showed him near the business school, but only for a few minutes before it shows him driving back towards Smithville.

When she had finished giving me the update, I asked her to tell Chris thanks again for suggesting that we put that tracking device on Dennis' truck. I told DB we would figure out what it all meant later when my phone showed an incoming call from Dean Smith. I quickly switched over to take his call.

"Hey, did I leave something in your office?"

"No, unfortunately, it's more serious than that. I got a call from the campus police chief."

Dean Smith relayed the events that caused the reason for the campus police chief to feel he needed to inform the Dean in case there was anything to it. There were two separate run-ins with a county judge named Dennis Johnson over his attempt to park in "no parking" areas. When told he could not park there, he was verbally abusive toward officers and ranted on about a sham award the President was presenting and how the person being honored was a fraud from the business school. He thought he could move a few blocks away and try again, but when immediately faced with more campus police, who were calling for more security, he quickly drove away.

The Dean explained, "this was just a courtesy call from the chief to inform me of the strange behavior and to make sure there was nothing more to it they need to know. Frank, do you think it's the guy who sent the threats earlier?"

"I do, and I'm going to do something about it. The last thing I want is for the University to be embarrassed. I am driving tomorrow to meet personally with him and address this directly and bring an end to this nonsense."

"Be careful."

We hung up and I tried to clear my mind as I headed toward the conference center restaurant to make reservations. Just thinking about sitting and catching up with Sara immediately put me in a much better mood.

FORTY-EIGHT

The big red truck sped down Texas Highway 71 eastward toward Bastrop and then on to Smithville. Most of the ride was spent letting off steam as an angry Dennis Johnson cussed himself for being so stupid and not realizing that campus security had increased greatly over the twenty-something years since he had been to the University campus, much of it due to 9-11. Thinking the campus police were just glorified parking meter attendants, he quickly realized they were trained law enforcement and security officials. After spending all that time to erase all the evidence that could be traced back to him, from hiding files on his computer to having the only copy of the information sitting next to him on the passenger's seat of this truck, he tossed it all into a storm drain as he hurriedly left campus. He would have to unlock his computer and re-create it. His plan would not go to waste as he vowed to himself to put an end to all this tomorrow. After doing the favor he promised to his constable buddy and serving papers in the morning, he would drive straight to the hotel where he knew Frank Travis was staying.

While the original plan of embarrassing Frank and bringing him down and doing so in front of all the UT and Texas state dignitaries had failed, there was a plan B. And, the Driskill Hotel will be a great place to end Frank's life and reputation.

FORTY-NINE

The conference center's restaurant is not unlike any you may find in an upscale hotel. It is well appointed, with works of art featuring Texas landscapes hanging on the walls. The lighting is dim, but the tables are lit well enough to read a menu. Texas-shaped centerpieces anchor each table and house multiple candles that outline the state's borders. I quickly find someone and make a reservation before going back to the hotel to make a few calls.

I arrive back at the conference center restaurant around 4 pm. Sara's meeting was scheduled to end at 4 pm, but if council meetings ran anything like my board meetings, it would go on another half hour or so. I didn't mind being early. The hostess walks me to a table located in the front corner where I can see the lobby to my left and the Bob Bullock Texas History Museum outside the windows to my right.

As I waited, the restaurant began to fill as meetings across the conference complex were ending and business associates were meeting for drinks before dinner. It wasn't long before I saw Sara approaching through the lobby. I stood so she could see me as she entered the restaurant. After a quick scan of the room, she saw me and the hostess brought her to the table.

I reach over and pull out her chair. "I am so glad we finally have a little time to catch up with each other. There is so much to talk about." I didn't want to seem overly anxious, and sat back down. I could not read her. She was acting somewhat guarded. You can't always put your finger on what it is exactly, but you always know when it's a little awkward.

"Me, too," replied Sara. "I have to be honest with you. I thought you may have blown me off for some reason after we saw each other last night. You said you would leave me a note of how to contact you." She smiled a little as she said this. "Not realizing you didn't know my married name is on me. I just wasn't thinking because the bellman had not only taken my bags but also had the room key."

We both laughed. We agreed that a glass of wine was appropriate to recognize and toast to her first meeting as a council member, and my President's Award. For now, we had no dinner plans, just a chance to talk.

We could have spent much more time just catching up. We talked about our careers and our current business priorities, and the travel necessary to make it all work. We spoke of our love for the University and how we had both remained involved over the years. And, after ordering a second glass of wine, we moved on to talk about our families. I explained my close calls with marriage, and how much I blamed myself for being too unavailable and not realizing it until it was too late. I told Sara about my relationship with Susan, and about how she just recently passed. For some reason, I teared up when talking about her death, something I had not done since the day I got the news of her death. I knew this was odd for me, but just chalked it up to the emotions of the day.

"I apologize. I don't mean to bring our conversation down like this." I explained. "She and I were very close and I guess I am still dealing with losing my best friend".

"Don't even think about apologizing," Sara said softly as she reached across the table and gently took my hand. Holding it, she placed her other hand over it and with both hands she gently squeezed mine and said, "I understand. And, I am just glad that after all these years you are comfortable enough to let your guard down and be honest with me".

Again, I felt her warmth and caring spirit flow through my entire body. "Thanks, Sara. Now, I've been doing a lot of the talking. Tell me about your husband and your family."

Sara suddenly let go of my hand, sat back and took a long, slow sip of wine. After a pause for reflection, she began to tell her story. Married for many years, never had children, loved to travel but work got in the way, a pancreatic cancer diagnosis, her husband's short but brutal fight against the deadly disease, and now she had been alone for these past seven years pouring herself into her career.

"Sara, I'm so sorry. That had to be awful for you as you watched him suffer. It sounds like he was a good man and y'all had a good life."

Sara continued, "It's been seven years and I have been able to move on. I've invested quite a bit more of my time into my firm, but I'm also now at a point where I am extremely confident in my team's ability to manage the operation and am looking to take my foot off the accelerator soon."

I could tell she was ready to get us off this topic and so I decided to take a big risk. "I know it's getting close to dinner, and I don't know if you have any plans, but would you want to join me for dinner tonight?"

If she said no, that was probably it—a nice time catching up between two old friends who would continue to go their own way. But, if she said yes...

"I would be happy to have dinner with you," Sara said smiling at the invitation. "I'll need some time back at the hotel to get ready. What do you say, about 7:30 pm?"

FIFTY

Z-Tejas is an Austin restaurant known for its southwestern-styled menu and its great atmosphere. Sitting atop the northwest hills overlooking Austin's Cat Mountain, it's a smart, casual setting—sport coat and button down with jeans and boots is not out of the ordinary for this constantly bustling environment. I valet park the rental car and walk around to open the door for Sara. It strikes me that she is stunningly elegant as she slides her legs out of the car and holds her hand out for me to assist. Her skin is a beautiful olive color, her nails manicured, and loose gold chain bracelets rest on her wrist. I couldn't help but notice that people waiting in line to enter the restaurant were all watching and couldn't take their eyes of her. I had on my cowboy boots, pressed jeans, and a heavily starched white button down. I looked like dozens of other men in the restaurant. But, Sara's beauty was stunning and her presence and style stood out among everyone.

FIFTY-ONE

"I see what you mean about this place," Sara said as they were seated. "What a great atmosphere with all these people really enjoying themselves."

"Wait until you taste their food. I think you will like it because its unique to Austin but has some traditional Southwestern flair, as well," I said as the hostess walked away and we were now alone with some time to ourselves. "I'd like to recommend we begin with a bottle of wine, and then start with one of my favorite appetizers here, the shrimp tostadas."

"That sounds great to me. What if we try that Texas wine you were telling me about earlier—was it called Grape Creek?" Sara inquired.

"That's a great suggestion, and we are in luck that we've come to this restaurant because it is one of only a few in Austin that serves Grape Creek wines. You can only get their wines at the winery in Fredericksburg, but they've begun these new relationships to test and see if they want to begin offering their wines to other restaurants."

After just a few minutes of talking about the restaurant and Austin's changes since we were in school, a 2007 Bellesimo, a cabernet sauvignon estate wine from Grape Creek, arrived at the table. The waitress poured two glasses.

"Cheers!" I said holding out my glass and tapping it against hers. I felt so relaxed and comfortable sitting with Sara now and wanted to hear everything she had to say.

We talked non-stop. Through the shrimp tostadas, through the pecan-crusted trout, and through the entire bottle of wine. We ordered coffees and knew the wait staff were anxious to move us out and seat waiting customers still crowding the front lobby. After talking about our careers, our current work, the President's Council appointment for her and the President's award for me, and touching on our relationships —my 'unlucky in love' stories and her husband's passing and how she's moved ahead from it, it was as if two good friends had reconnected.

OPPOSITE DIRECTIONS

I think in my heart, I was hoping for more. But, reconnecting with a friend like Sara was terrific even though neither of us brought up the subject of our decision to break off our college relationship once I graduated and moved across the county. I could not tell if she wanted more, and I was unsure enough that I was resigned to let her go again. She had an early flight to NYC in the morning. I had an early morning drive to Smithville before catching an afternoon flight to Portland. Once again, we were heading in opposite directions.

FIFTY-TWO

I pull up to the Driskill Hotel. The valet meets me as I walk around the back and over to open Sara's door. I make it around just in time to reach out my hand and help Sara out of the car and up the steps to the hotel's front doors. Once up the steps, she did not let go of my hand until we reached the revolving door. I knew my feelings for Sara were real.

"I had a great time tonight," Sara said as we walked into the lobby. "I have not felt this good in a long time."

She turns to face me, grabs both of my hands in hers, and pulls me closer. "I have thought of you often since losing my husband. I had no idea I would ever see you again. The nice boy I met while we were students has become a wonderful man. I will miss you." She reaches up with her arms and places them around my shoulders. She pulls me even closer and she stands on her toes to give me a gentle kiss on the lips. Then, as I expected her to pull away, another longer and intimate kiss. "Maybe one day our lives will slow down and we will be able to spend more time together. Thank you for a wonderful evening. Let's stay in touch." she said as she stepped back and smiled broadly. Just like that, she was off to the elevator and her room. I just stood there, speechless and trying to figure out what had just happened. This woman was a pure class act.

I felt a tear begin to form at the thought of not seeing Sara again. I quickly looked around to see if anyone noticed. I was happy to have reconnected with a very dear friend, but was also sad to think our lives just didn't seem to work together.

FIFTY-THREE

"DB, as always, I appreciate your great work," I said as we were about to end our daily briefing call. "I also want to thank you again for making these travel arrangements to where I can drive down to Smithville and meet with Dennis to see what his problem is, and then I have an appointment to try to wrap up work on Susan's estate".

I am about to hang up and DB interrupts. "Well, aren't you going to tell me more about yesterday?"

"Oh, of course," I said. "It was a beautiful setting and a truly special ceremony. The President Council members all said a lot of nice things as they presented me with the award".

"That's great. And, please forgive me. You know I am proud of your receiving such a prestigious award, but I was really asking about your evening with Sara." DB was great at cutting to the chase, even if it was personal. She knew she was one of the only people I could confide in.

"DB, I don't know. You know my track record with relationships. It was like two people who have known each other forever and had just not seen each other in a while. We were comfortable to talk about our lives, both business and personal. I feel like there was maybe a little spark. I think she felt the same way. But, maybe we are both too cautious because as we talked about our schedules and plans we realized that we are just going in too many different directions. We ended the evening saying good-bye and hoping our paths may cross again in the future." I left out the deep emotions I felt when said we said good-bye and kissed. I knew DB would have more questions than I had answers.

DB knows me too well. She heard something in my voice that sounded like maybe I am holding back. "Listen Frank, there was excitement in your voice yesterday when you told me a about your plans to meet Sara for dinner. Now, you sound like you are trying to hide or avoid something. Remember what you told me when you returned from your vacation in Hawaii?" DB said as she reminded me of my self-assessment of my failed relationships and how I had pledged to focus more and make more of an effort, if and when I found the right person, since I wanted to share my life with someone.

"Remember, this is the woman you have spent your life comparing all others to and wondering what if," DB continued. And she was right. I needed to figure out my feelings, and then see about figuring out Sara's. I did not need to just sit here and see what happens. I needed to make something happen. DB also remembered what I had told her about Jenny, the wise woman I met at Buzz's in Kailua. "It's not always what's next, it's what's now".

FIFTY-FOUR

Sara slept in and ordered room service. There was no way she was going to go down to the Driskill's breakfast area after she had been up most of the night. Her kiss, especially the second one to say good-bye was Sara's way of trying to gauge her feelings for Frank. Was she just excited to see and catch up with a good friend from the past, or was she really feeling something much more? Something she had not felt since losing her husband seven years ago. That kiss was a lot more than she had expected. Why had she said good-bye and left so quickly? Did she give Frank enough time to express his feelings—if he had them for her? Or, was he just being nice and was he okay with making a connection with an old friend?

She cancelled her early morning flight. To help clear her mind she scheduled a mid-morning meeting with her realtor to go look at some of the potential homes around West Austin and Lake Travis. Acting on her plan to move to Austin, maybe she could take her mind off of last night.

FIFTY-FIVE

You stupid idiot! Dennis gripes to himself as he pulls out of his driveway. A thick, pre-dawn fog blankets the area making anything outside the illumination of his headlights invisible. Continuing the scolding he is pouring out on himself, *If I hadn't tossed the folder and flash drive into the storm drain as I was being chased off campus, I wouldn't be up at this ridiculous hour of the morning driving in this mess with my head pounding from last night's drinking binge.* He laughs out loud, *who am I kidding—every night is a binge and every morning, no matter what time I get up, is head-pounding punishment.*

Dennis navigates carefully down Main Street before turning and entering the narrow alley behind his office. Parked close to a single, flickering lamp that hangs precariously above the back entrance to his office, he fumbles for his keys as he walks to open the backdoor. Across the way through the fog, he notices the lights from Johnny Lawson's auto repair shop come on. Somebody else is getting an early start today.

Entering the old building and its hallway that leads to his office, he sets down the folder he is carrying on the seat of his desk chair and walks back to the break room to make coffee. Settling in behind his desk, stopping only to grab more coffee, he works diligently covering his tracks and hiding all the things that could serve as potential evidence against him. Focused and riding a caffeine buzz, he works on his third cup of coffee. Time passes quickly and he fails to notice Tammy's arrival until the lights in the lobby go on. Tammy walks directly to his office and stands in the doorway. He had hoped to be done and out of the office by the time she arrived.

"Well, well, well! What is this?! I can't remember the last time you beat me into the office—because there isn't a last time. You're never here this early. What are you up to?"

Startled, but trying his best to hide it, Dennis quickly closes his desk drawer and browser tabs. "Good morning, 'Miss Nosey'. If you have to know, I have some prep to do for a meeting I have in Austin later today after I serve that summons this morning. I'll be heading to Austin after lunch."

"Sure thing, boss," Tammy says skeptically and with a heavy dose of sarcasm as she walks away to get some coffee and straighten up the office before they officially opened in a few minutes.

Dennis removes the flash drive from his computer, places it into his front shirt pocket, and finishes off his coffee before heading out. If he hadn't destroyed the drive he took to Austin yesterday in his failed attempt to blackmail Frank, he wouldn't have had to come in and do this all over again. "Tammy, I'm headed to Rex Water's place to deliver this summons. I'll stop back by the office to check in before driving to Austin."

As Dennis is walking out, Tammy sees that he is taking a gun with him, "What's up with the gun? You're not expecting trouble, are you?"

"It's just a precaution. If nothing else, just to scare Rex if he gets belligerent about being served." Dennis knew Tammy well enough to assume that if she noticed him with a gun she may ask, so he was prepared with the story about Rex, even though the gun was definitely intended for Frank.

FIFTY-SIX

DB and I are on our daily call taking care of only business she deems urgent while I'm driving down Highway 71. Today's agenda is short. I have to concentrate on how to handle confronting Dennis. It is priority number one for today. I'm just about to hang up when DB says, "Hey, hold on just a second. I just got a text from Chris. He says the tracker shows the red truck just outside of town. It appears to be driving down a small county road. Frank, it looks like Dennis is not at his office."

"Tell Chris thanks for the heads up and to let us know when the truck heads back to town. You can text me when you hear back from him. In the meantime, I'll go to Dennis' office, see if I can get any information out of his assistant, and wait for him to return. If he comes back here, I want to surprise him, not the other way around."

"Got it. I'll give Chris a call and let him know you are there for the next hour or so. I'll ask him to be alert over the next couple of hours so you can get real time information if possible."

Surprisingly, for a small town, I notice as I cross the river bridge that there were a number of cars moving around town as everyone was getting their day started. We are all moving a little slower due to the fog, but it was burning off and visibility was improving slightly. One of the beauties of a small town is that there is no rush hour traffic, no long lines waiting at the traffic light, and no fight for a parking space. I pull up in front of the county judge's office, step outside, look around, and then walk inside.

FIFTY-SEVEN

"Hello! I'm Frank Travis and I'm here to see Judge Dennis Johnson."

Tammy laughs. She hadn't heard anyone use Dennis' title of Judge in a while. "He is out right now, but I expect him back in about 30 minutes. You're welcome to wait if you'd like. Can I get you a cup of coffee?"

"Thanks. I'll take you up on that coffee and wait for him to get back".

I look around the office. I smile at the Hope Floats movie posters, a point of pride for all of us who loved that Hollywood chose our small town to film a major movie. The photo of the FFA student draping a blue ribbon across their steer reminds me of high school and raising animals for the annual livestock show as part of the Ag classes. Before too much nostalgia sets in, Tammy walks over with a steaming mug of black coffee. The mug has a slogan written across it, 'Smithville, a small town with a big heart'.

"Here you go. Tell me, is there anything I can do to help you since Dennis is not here?"

"No, I'm just an old friend stopping in to see him."

"Frank Travis, hmm, I don't recall hearing your name from him, but it does sound familiar." Just then it hit her—this is the guy everyone in town always blames for the railroad museum accident. She tried not to show it, but could tell he knew from her expression she knew who he was. She had moved to town long after Frank had left, but the stories live on in small towns. With the recent death of his sister, all the old stories had been circulating again. "I'm sorry, I remember now and I am very sorry about Susan's passing. She was a sweetheart."

"Yes, yes she was. Thank you for the kind words." After an awkward silence, I asked to use the phone. "I have an appointment with Susan's attorney and want to let him know I'm here in town and will be heading over to his office to see him at the top of the hour."

"Sure, use this phon...." The office phone rang and Tammy answered. As she engaged with the person calling, she held her hand over the speaker and whispered, "This may take a while. Why don't you use the phone in Dennis' office."

FIFTY-EIGHT

The red truck turns off of the highway just past Oak Hill Cemetery and onto a weathered, one-lane country road that was once paved but is now full of cracks and pot holes. After passing by a newly-built brick home, a couple of mobile homes across the road, and a large open pasture, the road turns into a gravel road for the next couple of miles. Just past a few ranch homes Dennis comes to a dead end. On the left, there is an old iron gate pushed open. A chain and open lock hang from one of the gate posts. On the right is a rodeo arena and barn with a sign suggesting it is used for training rodeo animals.

Dennis turns left through the open gate, crosses the cattle guard, then proceeds to drive up a dirt road that winds around scrub oaks and mesquites and finally ends at Rex Waters' trailer. Deep in thought about what he is going to do later in the day, and how he will have his revenge against Frank, he realizes he is not paying attention to the task at hand. It is time to focus on how to make this summons as easy as possible.

Rex has a tough guy reputation. He is a former SWAT officer who got kicked out due to rumors he was dealing arms on the side. It was never confirmed but the rumor stayed with him. A Viet-Nam vet, he is also rumored to have PTSD-type outbursts of anger. However, everything seems to be rumors and Dennis found no actual incidents on his record. So, he figures, this will be as simple as maybe getting cussed out.

After sitting there for a minute, it is obvious that Rex is not coming out to greet him. Dennis gets out of the truck to go knock on the door. Walking around an old rusted lawn chair and past knee-high weeds, he climbs the wooden stairs of the detached front porch that wobbles on the uneven ground fronting the mobile home. It has a few loose boards but is sturdy enough. Dennis knocks. No answer. He knocks louder this time. No answer.

FIFTY-NINE

I can't believe this stroke of good luck, I'm saying to myself as I walk into Dennis' office to use his phone. While Tammy is distracted talking on the phone, I quickly insert the flash drive into Dennis' computer. I hear it engage to plant its virus. The next time anyone logs in, the virus will activate and erase the hard drive. I quickly remove the flash drive and am putting it into my pocket when Tammy appears at the door.

"I thought you wanted to make a call."

"Well, I uh, I couldn't figure out how to dial out", I said just making up whatever came into my mind and not knowing whether she saw me take the flash drive out of his pc.

"Oh, sorry about that. Just dial 9 to get an outside line. I'm not sure why we even have this in such a small office. It's something headquarters wants everyone to have, whether we need it or not."

Phew, that was close. I pulled out his card, dialed the attorney's office, and let him know I would be there shortly. I accomplished a big part of what I wanted, to make sure there was no evidence, no more pictures, and no more threats. I asked Tammy to let Dennis know I had been there, hoping that knowing the fact I was going to confront him may intimidate him and stop him from his strange behavior. Thanking Tammy once again I leave to drive three blocks to the other end of Main Street to meet with Susan's attorney.

SIXTY

"Rex, this is Dennis Johnson, the county judge. Come out and let's talk." Dennis is starting to wonder if anyone is home when he hears movement that sounds like someone is inside. The sounds get louder like someone is coming to the door, so Dennis steps back. Suddenly the door swings open.

In a flash—the barrel of a shotgun is a foot away from his chest, an explosion of fire and smoke leaving the barrel and knocking him backwards followed by a deafening sound—Dennis Johnson was dead before he hit the ground, rolling down the loose boards of the porch steps. The force of the blast leaves him lying on the ground surrounded by weeds and next to the rusting old lawn chair.

Not more than a couple of minutes later, having heard the sound of a gunshot, a neighbor from across the fence runs over, crawls through the barbed wire fence, and runs toward the home to see if his neighbor Rex is okay. He doesn't find Rex, but finds Dennis, dead on the ground. He barely recognizes him through all the blood, but sees Dennis' truck in the front of the mobile home. Dialing 911, he asks for police and an ambulance. Being out in the country, and knowing it will take a little while for them to arrive. He begins to look around. He stands up on the red truck's running board to look inside. He sees a gun and a box of bullets. Wrapped around the box was a piece of white duct tape with something written on it. Reaching in he picks up the box of ammo, and is able to read what is written on the tape—-Special Delivery - Frank Travis.

SIXTY-ONE

"Well, that should just about wrap it up", Susan's attorney says as he hands me the final paper that needs my signature. "I appreciate you coming down personally and helping take care of all this. I knew Susan for more than 20 years, and I know what a special person she was to everyone in this town. You know, small towns are very close-knit groups. Many times, we have people move in from the city, like I did, and the locals fear that we want to change things and make this great small town into another version of the city they just left. And, for some people that is true. But in my case and many others it is not. Your sister really took me under her wing and helped pave the way for the people here to accept me. She taught me how to not bring the big city to Smithville, but to blend in and become part of Smithville. My law practice would not have been successful without Susan's kindness and guidance. I will always be indebted to her."

"Thank you for sharing that story with me", I replied. "Susan was my best friend. And, I realize that she was also a lot of people's best friend. I miss her."

We stood up and shook hands. I walk out into bright sunshine that has replaced the morning fog. I take a long look up one side of Main Street and down the other. Boy, has it changed from the days I rode my bike to Trousdale's Pharmacy to read comic books and drink a malt from the soda fountain. I walk past storefronts of the former newspaper office and barber shop to the new sports bar that has been a highlight and huge success for the town. Named for and run by a very popular coach, and the brother of a close friend and classmate, I peek through the window to look inside. It will not open until noon, but I am able to see posted on the walls all the photos of Smithville's student athletes, band members, twirlers and cheerleaders from throughout the decades. There I am with my teammates and friends. And, there is Susan in photos with many of her friends. An important part of our lives was growing up in a town like Smithville and it was represented on those walls.

Stopping to grab an early lunch on my way out of town at another business owned and operated by dear old friends, I enjoy some of the best BBQ in Central Texas. It is rated one of the best in Texas annually by many magazine polls. However, people didn't need magazine ratings, all you had to do is taste it to know it was special. These friends are among the few loyal friends I still had here.

SIXTY-TWO

I'm walking across the gravel parking lot to my car which I parked in the back under the shade of a centuries old live oak. I wonder if I should stop by to see if Dennis is back at his office when I notice a red pickup truck pulling out of the gas station across the street. It speeds across the gravel parking lot leaving a trail of dust behind it. I flinch as it comes to an abrupt stop next to me. It's Little Roger Daniels.

"I'm glad I caught you. I went by Dennis' office and Tammy told me you were in town. I drove around to see if you were still here and thought I missed you. Then I saw you walking to the back here where the pit is as I was filling up with gas."

He went on to give me the news. Dennis had been shot and killed. I was in shock, and I'm pretty sure he was too because he didn't take a breath and stop talking for 5 minutes. I finally interrupted.

"Roger, thanks for letting me know. You told me that he was upset with me for some reason. Then he contacted my office acting very strange. So, I came down to meet with him this morning to find out what the deal was and..."

Roger interrupted me this time. "Look, I think I know. I don't have much time to explain because I am supposed to be on my way to the police station to file a report since I'm a witness. Before I go, I have to tell you something. After I heard a shot, I went across the fence to see what happened. I found Dennis dead on the ground. While I was waiting for the police to arrive, I looked around and found this in Dennis' truck"

He handed me the box of ammo with my name on it.

"I'm not certain, but it looks like you may have been in some real danger. It may have been to scare you, but in Dennis' frame of mind it could have been that he intended to kill you. I am going to give you this box but ask you not to say anything. Dennis was weird with some problems, and his drinking made it worse, but lots of people respect him around here –he's won three consecutive elections—and it will do no good now to ruin his and his family and friend's reputations."

He went on to give me a quick summary of what he had heard from others about what Dennis had told his drinking buddies about me, about Susan, and just ridiculous teenage jealousies that took a life of their own as his drinking had become worse. And, of course I understood about keeping a secret, and preserving reputations for those still here in a small town. I appreciated it since for years I have been doing the same for Ben and Reggie and their families. It turns out that Little Roger and I had even more in common than our sports careers.

"Roger, I understand completely and will keep this to myself. I agree, there is no need to punish Dennis even more than what just happened to him. You are a good man."

Still in shock, I get into my car and drive back over the river bridge toward Austin. I have to call DB right away.

SIXTY-THREE

"Good morning! Thanks for picking me up and for choosing a few homes to look at this morning. I appreciate you setting these up with such short notice." Sara explains her schedule and timeline as they leave the hotel and drive around the block to get back onto Congress Avenue.

"My pleasure. It's nice to meet you in person. Kelsey has told me so much about you." Anne, the Austin realtor, is Kelsey's aunt and has lived in Austin her entire life. She thinks she knows just where to find what Sara is looking for in a home.

"Kelsey is not just one of my top execs, but she is also a good friend," explains Sara as she gives Kelsey's aunt a quick history of their work together.

Driving down Sixth Street and over to Enfield, then down Cherry Lane and eventually over to Scenic Drive, we look at homes along the shores of Lake Austin. The homes and neighborhoods are absolutely beautiful along this stretch of Lady Bird Lake which is part of the Colorado river that runs through downtown Austin. But Sara's mind is set on a hilltop view next to water and there were no hills on this stretch of shoreline. So, they take Mount Bonnell Drive to Ranch Road 2222 and drive to Lakeway where Sara hopes to find the perfect home for her move to Austin.

Nestled in the western corner of Travis county, Lakeway is a gateway to the beautiful Texas Hill Country. The town sits on the south shore of Lake Travis, about twenty miles from Austin. It began as a resort community with world-class golf and tennis facilities, along with a private airport and marina. It became so popular that today it is no longer a calm, retirement and second-home community but a bustling little city that has doubled in population each decade since the turn of the century.

Driving the popularity, and piquing Sara's interest, is Lake Travis. One of seven in the Highland Lakes chain, it serves primarily as flood control, but this lake has become one of Texas' most popular for recreation. It's one of the state's largest, and its limestone cliffs and beds create clear azure water that matches the sky, something that is rare for Texas lakes.

The first home Anne shows Sara is high on a hilltop, with access to the lake just an elevator ride below to a boat dock. The home is positioned on a large lot with greenbelts on two sides providing privacy and a natural setting. A nearby marina and Lakeway's World of Tennis resort are just a couple of the many amenities and the lake view is spectacular.

"There is enough room on this lot to add on a couple of rooms that I'd like to have. I think this may be the one. The house needs some work, not much, but I want to add some outdoor living space, a workout room, and a large conference room for when my executive team meets here," Sara explained to her realtor.

With the realtor's help and her longtime Austin connections, Sara is able to put in an offer by phone as they drive back to Austin. "Thanks again so much for helping me find such a great place. If you will drop me off at the UT campus, I'll find my way back to the hotel after I pick up something from the UT President's office," Sara asked while acknowledging that she would be in touch before she flew out later in the day.

"Kelsey, your aunt just dropped me off. She is a wonderful person and real estate agent. Thanks for asking her to help me."

"I'm glad she was helpful. Did you see anything you like?"

"Not only did I find something I liked, I put an offer down just 30 minutes ago."

"Wow, that's great Sara. It looks like your timetable to move may happen a little quicker than you were planning."

"Yes, although if the offer is accepted, I do want to have some work done on it before moving. But, even with that, it looks like it will happen sooner that I thought. With that in mind, please pass this along to the rest of the team. I'll give you all more details when I get back."

SIXTY-FOUR

"DB, you will not believe what happened this morning!" I give her a complete run down—from the ease of planting the virus to erase Dennis' computer hard drive to the shocking event of his murder. I explain the box of bullets that Roger had found and given me, asking for strict confidence.

"Unbelievable! I can't even get my head around all this. I'm glad you are safe. This was a real threat. I'm just shaking to think what could have happened. We really misjudged the situation."

"Yeah, I think so too. I didn't take the threat as seriously as I should have taken it. It's pretty clear now that confronting him was not going to be a good plan. Please call Chris, fill him in, and please thank him for me until I have a chance to give him a call myself."

"I'll do that right away. It's all so shocking. It does not feel real right now. And, now you have another secret to keep—how crazy is that?"

"Thank you, DB. I now realize I put you at risk and I am sorry. I was careless and I definitely owe you." I hang up and can still feel adrenaline pumping through my body as I tried to make sense of all this.

I usually enjoy the hour-long drive back to Austin by listening to some of my favorite music, but today I ride in silence. Even with all the drama surrounding Dennis, my mind, no matter how hard I try to redirect it keeps going back to Sara's kiss. How that's possible after having my life in danger, I have no idea.

I checked out of the hotel earlier this morning and the rental car isn't due back for another couple of hours. I decide to drop by campus, grab a taco, and kill some time.

Parking on campus is always an issue, so all I can find is a space in a distant lot near the stadium. I enjoy the long walk. Students blanket the campus going to and from classes. By the time I arrive at central campus the Tower bells are ringing. A sea of students moves in every direction and clogs the mall surrounding Old Main as they change classes. In no hurry, I carefully dodge in and around them, and ease my way up the steps to enjoy the view of the magnificent Tower set against a sapphire sky now littered with hundreds of cotton ball clouds. You know what they say about Texas weather—if you don't like it, just stick around, it will change again soon. I hang back to observe, but to also let the crowd thin out, and then look toward the West Mall where I can see the 'tablers' out in force.

Suddenly I freeze. *Is this real? Is that her? I can't believe it. It's Sara.* My reaction tells me all I need to know—this is not just another coincidence that I can let pass. There can be no more "what if?" for me. On a scale of 1 to 10, this day is 10-plus crazy and only getting crazier.

I stand at a distance and watch her talk with students at one of the tables. Thoughts fly through my mind. Wasn't she was supposed to fly out early this morning? What is she doing here? Then, almost as if she feels my presence, Sara turns and sees me standing there.

Without even a brief pause, I see her smile and begin walking with a purpose. I, too, begin walking with a purposeful and direct stride. We are moving in opposite directions, but this time we are going directly toward each other.

We embrace—a meaningful hug—and then stand holding each other's hands and looking at each other. "What a wonderful surprise!" I finally blurt out. "I thought you had flown out of Austin early this morning."

"Something just didn't feel right about the way we left things last night. I had a difficult time sleeping and so I had a lot of time to think. I cancelled my flights, called my realtor, and decided to stay here and try and find a home to buy. I have decided to make the move to Austin right away. I put in an offer on a home earlier today." Sara was about to continue, but I interrupted.

"Wow, I'm happy you found a place here so quickly. I have to tell you, I also had a sleepless night. After the morning I've had, including meeting with my sister's attorneys, I decided to make a last-minute stop by the campus before flying out. Now, I am so glad that I did. Last night was amazing. I have not felt that way in a long time. I'd really like to spend some more time together."

"I feel the same way," replied Sara. "I thought maybe I was making too much of last night, but us meeting here under these circumstances has to be more than just a coincidence."

We were still holding each other's hands. We have each other now, and don't want to let go.

DANNY INGRAM

In case you didn't know
Baby I'm crazy 'bout you
And I would be lying if I said
That I could live this life without you...
You had my heart a long, long time ago
In case you didn't know...Brett Young, In Case You Didn't Know

SIXTY-FIVE – One Year Later

It's been a year of changes. I moved to Austin. It's allowed Sara and I to spend time and get reacquainted. It has been better than I could have imagined. Sharing each other's stories—the triumphs and especially the losses—has brought us closer. And all of this in a year where so much has happened that continues to change our lives.

I resigned my role as CEO, leaving the company on great terms and in good hands with my hand-picked successor. I started my own consulting firm, convincing DB to join me as my Chief of Staff. She has always help run my business, so I thought she deserved the title and salary that was appropriate for all she did. Now, she manages the business operations and our small but growing staff of six.

For years, Dean Smith has tried to recruit me to serve as a faculty member of the business school. I finally took him up on his offer. I teach 3 days a week on campus, which gives me time to consult and work along with DB to grow our new business. My travel schedule is also a lot more manageable. Sara has also cut back on her schedule. We have both adjusted to our new, slower pace. We are still focused on our work, but we enjoy the time we have when not working.

Last year, I told myself I would not come back to Smithville to visit Susan's grave, but here I am. And why not? After giving it more thought since I moved to Austin, it's only logical. It's only an hour's drive. It is a great little town full of memories I have of Susan and I growing up. And, I realized that all the drama over the past year with Susan's passing and then the bizarre threats from Dennis Johnson are not reasons to avoid Smithville. It's my hometown, and I really don't care if people want to hold onto what happened so long ago. I have reconnected with some good friends and have been back four or five times over the year.

So, here I sit, on the small stone bench next to Susan's headstone. I run down the latest news for her. Rex is still on the run and has not been found. He bolted immediately after he shot and killed Dennis, and with his military training and skills he has been able to disappear so far. The investigation found that he was cooking meth in his trailer, evidently very high while doing so, and got spooked by Dennis' knock on his door. Seems like Dennis was in the wrong place at the wrong time. Besides the gun in Dennis' truck, the only other thing they found were pieces of a flash drive lying next to him on the ground. Parts of it were found in his shirt pocket. They tried to piece it together to see if it held any other clues to why this happened, but to no avail.

On a brighter note, I tell her things are great with Sara. Y'all would get along so well. I really wish the two of you had been able to meet and get to know each other.

And, importantly for you and me, the secret is safe. Ben and Reggie, along with their families, remain honored and respected citizens of this community.

I leave the cemetery after walking over to pay my respects at the gravesites of Reggie and Ben. I still miss them. I dial the phone to DB as I pull out onto the highway. I fill her in on what I've learned about Rex and Dennis.

"It's definitely a sad ending for a sad man, but our secret remains safe. "

"Which one?" DB jokes. "Frank, I need to let you go. I've got the staff meeting in a few minutes and need to make sure the agendas are printed. I'll talk to you tomorrow."

There's not much traffic, which is very unusual for the drive between Smithville and Austin, and onto Lakeway. I make it back a little earlier than I thought I would.

As I turn my Highlander into the newly paved circle drive in front of Sara's home, I marvel at what a makeover she has done with this property. Landscaped to match the rocky, limestone cliffs along the road leading to her place, the home sits on a promontory point overlooking the lake. It blends into the greenbelt and space surrounding the home. The extra rooms Sara added extend her views from the pool deck and veranda, and rock pathways make their way around the home and into greenbelt trails that traverse the shoreline.

Sara is still on a conference call when I arrive, so I find my way to the veranda and sit on one of the two chairs we often use to watch sunsets. She has also created a beautiful outdoor living space—staring off to the north and west at the magnificent hill country, the lake, and the distant hills that host many wonderful sunsets. I take the chilled bottle of *Angela's Wish*, a local Stonehouse Winery favorite we have discovered, and pour two glasses, placing them and the bottle on the small table between our chairs.

The more time we have spent together this past year, the closer we have become. The past couple of months, with Sara moving into her new home, we have become almost inseparable. Only business trips have kept us from seeing each other every day. We are on the same page on most things, even if we have different approaches. In that way, we complement each other. From the silly to the profound. From squeezing the toothpaste from the middle of the tube or more neatly from the bottom to understanding that either a direct or indirect approach can get you to the same destination. Our values line up, and we understand the role faith plays in our lives. We have fallen deeply in love.

"Frank, sorry I'm running a little late."

"No worries, I just got here. Cheers!" I say handing her one of the glasses of wine I poured.

After some time to relax, enjoy the wine, and catch up on the day's activities, I pour us another glass. I turn and face Sara.

"This past year, with all the changes, but most of all the time we have been able to spend together, has been one of the happiest times of my life. I always thought I had a good life. I had my work and my freedom, I had my name and good reputation. But I realize that still, there was a sorrow and emptiness. You have changed that."

A small tear begins to form in Sara's eye. She sits up on the edge of her chair and stares into Frank's brown eyes. "With this love we have, I've found strength I never knew I had. It's like nothing I have ever known. There were days upon days after my husband died, when I felt that the world was against me. But I kept on believing that this day would come. "

I move closer to Sara, entranced by her sparkling blue eyes. "After our parents died, Susan and I wanted to stay together and keep a home, but it wasn't. As much as we leaned on each other, it wasn't really truly a home. We knew it, but figured that's what life had dealt us. Now, with you, I realize what home could be like. "

Sara slowly stands and takes Frank by the hand. "This love, like I said, is like nothing I have ever known. Take my hand, Frank, I'm taking you home.

The End

www.ingramcontent.com/pod-product-compliance
Lightning Source LLC
Chambersburg PA
CBHW051215160726
47994CB00002B/617